DOCTOR DW WHO

SYSTEM WIPE

Oli Smith

The Doctor finds himself trapped in the virtual world of Parallife. As he tries to save the inhabitants from being destroyed by a deadly virus, Amy and Rory must fight to keep the Doctor's body in the real world safe from the mysterious entity known as Legacy . . .

For Emma, who likes this one best.

DOCTOR ⟨DW⟩ WHO

SYSTEM WIPE

Oli Smith

Cover illustrated by Paul Campbell

BBC Children's Books
Published by the Penguin Group
Penguin Books Ltd, 80 Strand, London, WC2R 0RL, England
Penguin Group (USA) Inc., 375 Hudson Street, New York 10014, USA
Penguin Books (Australia) Ltd, 250 Camberwell Road, Camberwell,
Victoria 3124, Australia (A division of Pearson Australia Group PTY Ltd)
Penguin Group (NZ), 67 Apollo Drive, Rosedale, North Shore
0632, New Zealand (A division of Pearson New Zealand Ltd)
Canada, India, South Africa
Published by BBC Children's Books, 2011
Text and design © Children's Character Books
The Good, the Bad and the Alien written by Colin Brake
System Wipe written by Oli Smith
001 – 10 9 8 7 6 5 4 3 2 1

ISBN – 978-14059-0-758-3

Mixed Sources
Product group from well-managed
forests and other controlled sources
www.fsc.org Cert no. SA-COC-1592
FSC © 1996 Forest Stewardship Council

Printed in Great Britain by Clays Ltd, St Ives plc

CONTENTS

The city was virtual.

But that doesn't mean it wasn't real.

Dubstep Towers hung in a neon-pink sky above the wireframe city below. The crowds of people hurrying through the outlined streets looked like pixels to Blondie – squares of colour, the building blocks of her world. She stood at the window of her penthouse apartment on floor 73, placed a hand against the glass and returned her gaze to the horizon.

Beyond the curving buildings and past the cubic city blocks, the darkness was coming. It was a sphere of pure black that extended both above and below the level of the ground and as it grew in size, its radius began to skim the yellow-lit suburbs.

The suburbs shattered. The roads and houses dissolved into a shower of computer code – carefully balanced strings of numbers and equations that held the world together. The glowing yellow pieces rose and flowed away from the advancing sphere, transforming into a tidal wave that sprayed the edges of the deep blue inner city. The yellow pixels mixed with the blue fragments, forming cool, green puddles on the streets before they were gathered up into the wave once more.

Blondie drew the blinds, unable to watch, and stepped over to the large four-poster bed that stood in the centre of the white-tiled room. Kneeling down, she pulled a large black trunk from beneath the bed and pressed her hand against the top. The cool dark material dissolved and Blondie smiled as the contents of the trunk reminded her of the adventures of her younger days.

Placed carefully amongst the protective folds of a crimson cloth was a sword. The ivory handle was sculpted to fit her palm and the perfectly balanced blade glowed with white electricity that matched Blondie's hair. She lifted it out of the trunk and flourished it with skill before slotting it neatly into the strap on her back. She pulled on a pair of blue boots that matched her blouse and took one last look at the flat that had been her home for Boss-knows how long. Behind the blinds, the soft patter of pixels began to sound against the glass – the wave was almost upon her.

Blondie opened the front door to the penthouse and looked down at the 200 metre drop below before stepping over the threshold. Her body twisted ninety degrees in the air, and the smooth wall of Dubstep Towers became the floor, as she began to walk down towards the street below. The building shuddered as the wave of destruction broke against the opposite side and Blondie began to run.

She couldn't fight the darkness on her own. She needed help.

CHAPTER 1
WORLD'S END

'It's the end of the world. Again,' said the Doctor.

'Again?' Rory made a face.

'When?' asked Amy. 'The buildings look like the kinda stuff you'd see in 2010.'

'Ha.' The Doctor laughed. 'That's the trouble with you born-in-the-twentieth-century types – you think it's only a matter of decades before your council estates and tower blocks are replaced with shiny domes and monorails and flying cars. But it's not. Buildings like this are renovated and repaired, they'll last for centuries.'

'Okay, so when is it?' Amy repeated.

'It's 2222 AD,' the Doctor answered. 'Like I said, end of the world.' He spread his arms and grinned as the group stopped to take in their surroundings.

All around them, the ruins of Chicago towered above their heads. Huge, broken skeletons of skyscrapers standing half-submerged amongst the vast folds of sand dunes. The dunes glowed white in the sunlight and faded to a cool grey in the giant shadows between the buildings. Beyond that, the desert stretched for miles, rolling hills of dust that rose and fell like a frozen sea towards the horizon.

'What happened?' Rory asked.

The Doctor flicked open his sonic screwdriver and pointed it towards the sky before examining the handle. He shrugged 'Dunno.'

'"Dunno"?' Rory repeated. 'What do you mean, "dunno"? It's the end of the world! Our whole world has been destroyed, and that didn't stick in your memory?'

The Doctor sighed. 'I can't keep track of everything. Earth gets blasted half a dozen times at least in its lifetime. Count yourself lucky,' he started jumping on the spot, 'at least the planet's still here this time.'

Amy reached out and closed her husband's open mouth. She turned to the Doctor, 'Could it be solar flares?' she asked. 'It's about the right era, isn't it?'

'Possibly.' The Doctor stuffed the sonic screwdriver back into his jacket pocket. 'The atmosphere's taken a beating, that's for sure.' He fished out a small white plastic bottle. 'Here, put this on – for protection.'

Rory inspected the bottle gingerly. 'What is it? Space cream?'

'Sunscreen. Your pasty complexions aren't going to last long without it.'

Amy snatched the bottle out of Rory's hand and started smearing it on immediately.

'And you tell me this now?! I've been out here nearly half an hour!'

'What about you?' Rory asked the Doctor.

The Doctor grinned and slipped on a pair of sunglasses. 'Sorted.'

It wasn't long before the relentless heat drove the group's exploration indoors. They blinked to adjust their eyes in the stifling shadows of one of the more intact skyscrapers. The Doctor's boots left prints in the dust as he stepped onto the green-tiled floor of a large, splintered entrance chamber.

'It's a block of flats.' Amy pointed behind a semi-circular reception desk to where a wide grid of mailboxes was screwed into the wall.

'In downtown, no less. Very posh.' The Doctor removed his shades and wiped them absent-mindedly on his shirtsleeves. Rory tried in vain to blow away the dust that had stuck to the suncream on his arm. His spluttering was loud in the heavy silence and Amy shot Rory a look as the Doctor pushed past her on his way towards the janitor's closet.

He yanked open the wooden door and stepped inside. A second later, the green bulb of the sonic screwdriver cast an eerie glow over the contents of the tiny closet.

'What are you looking for?' Amy asked.

'A power source.' The Doctor's voice was muffled in the gloom. 'Rory, be a good fella and thump that desk for me, would you?'

Rory raised his eyebrows but did as he was told. Gathering his shirt-cuff into his palm, he wiped a sleeve across the surface of the desk before poking it with a finger.

'I said thump, not poke.'

Rory patted the desk again.

'Oh, let me do it.' Amy strode forward and brought a fist down hard on the glossy surface. The desk sprang into life. With a small chime it began to display large rectangles of data – resident's details, room numbers, virtual post-it notes, all arranging themselves around Amy's hand.

'It's a table-computer!' Rory exclaimed.

The Doctor emerged from the closet, slapping the sonic screwdriver closed in his palm. 'It's a Desktop,' he said with a grin. Pushing between the pair he rubbed his thumbs over his fists and examined the scrolling readouts before him. Then he scratched at his nose as his other hand began jabbing at the screen in a dizzying flurry of movements. The readouts changed; colours and text flashing across the faces of Amy and Rory as if they were lit by a disco ball.

'What are you looking for?' Rory asked.

'The bills,' the Doctor replied. 'Somewhere in this building, something is still switched on. I picked up the power reading when we were outside but it's too faint for me to pinpoint with the sonic. I reckon whichever apartment it is must have racked up a pretty hefty electricity bill over the centuries. Hopefully that should tell us where the reading's coming from.'

'Is that why we came here?' Rory asked.

'It is now.'

The Desktop made one final chime and the Doctor raised his hand from the surface screen. 'Floor 48, apartment 23B.'

Amy eyed the grand main staircase, and pointed a finger. 'Are you expecting me to climb forty-eight times those?' she asked.

The Doctor shrugged. 'If you want. I was planning on taking the lift.'

CHAPTER 2
LINK-UP

'If it's the end of the world, how come the lifts still work?' Rory asked, as the Doctor checked his watch. The blue numbers that seemed to be projected across the top of the door were rising painfully slowly. So was the temperature inside the cramped metal lift.

'It's one of the basic rules of the universe, isn't it?' Amy threw him a wink. 'Things only work when you don't need them anymore.'

Rory nodded wisely. 'Like when our train broke down on the way to that concert.'

'You mean that gig,' said Amy.

'Gig, concert, what's the difference? It's still people playing music in front of other, slightly less sweaty people.'

'Gig sounds cooler.'

'It doesn't matter how cool it sounds. They're still sweaty.'

Amy sighed.

The Doctor stroked his bow tie. 'I'm sweaty and cool,' he declared.

'Urgh.'

'Aaaand we're here.' The Doctor announced, hopping out and into a hallway. Once it must have been decorated in a deep shade of red, but now the paintwork had faded to a rusty brown. 'Thank heavens for that. Remind me never to listen to you two talk about normal stuff again. Boooring!'

Sheepishly, the pair followed him down the corridor as the Doctor checked off the room numbers with a wag of his finger. Amy felt a weird sensation through her shoes and looked down to see the carpet crumbling away beneath her weight. Her feet left red footprints in the powder-snow of the worn out carpet.

'It's spooky,' she said. 'When you go to rundown places back home you expect them to be full of bugs and rats and mice and spiders and . . . more bugs,' she finished. 'But there's nothing here. Not a single living soul in the whole wide world.'

'Peaceful, isn't it?' the Doctor called over his shoulder cheerfully. 'Ah ha! 23B!' He stopped in front of a blank wooden door whose number he had deduced by examining the numbers of the doors either side. Grabbing the handle, he barged through.

And nearly fell to his death.

Amy grabbed him just in time. She shielded her eyes against the sudden shaft of sunlight and hauled him back over the threshold. He dropped onto the floor of the hallway with a thump.

The Doctor sat up immediately and stared in confusion at his legs as they dangled over the broken edges of the floorboards. He looked down at the steep drop below.

The entire eastern side of the building had been torn away by a force that must have been so powerful it sent shivers down Amy's spine. Her eyes adjusted to the light and she peered over the edge. The concrete skeleton of the building had crumbled to reveal a series of sharp metal supports nearly twenty storeys down. They were positioned exactly where the Doctor would have landed. Her stomach turned at the thought.

'But, I don't understand!' the Doctor finally found his voice. 'Where's 23B?'

'Er, here?' came a small cough from behind them.

Rory was standing on the opposite side of the hallway. He pointed at the number on the door next to him. 23B.

The Doctor cleared his throat. 'Ah, right, thanks.' He jumped quickly to his feet and began patting his trousers down enthusiastically. 'I must have confused "apartment 23B" with "creaky door of deathly death". Ah well, no harm done.' He straightened up and placed a hand on Amy's shoulder.

'Thanks.' he mouthed, and for a second Amy thought she saw a flicker of fear being blinked away behind his deep green eyes. Then it passed, and the blustering madman she knew so well returned once more. This time when the Doctor grabbed the door handle, he opened it considerably more slowly.

The door swung gently open to reveal a surprisingly small apartment considering the faded luxury of the hallway. Inside was a basic desk and chair. They were tucked neatly in one corner against a small, frosted window. To the right, behind a pokey bathroom, was an unmade bed that looked like it would crumble to ash if anyone so much as breathed on it.

Rory looked disappointed. 'I thought this

place was meant to be posh?'

'It's the location you pay for, not the size.' It only took the Doctor a couple of steps to reach the desk. He ran a finger across the surface, tracing a zigzag in the dust and a small blue light appeared in the centre of the Desktop. With a smooth whirr, a strange device appeared to unfold itself from the desk. It resembled a stylish doctor's stethoscope. A small wishbone shape was attached to one end, and the spine of the device curved up before straightening out to meet the light.

'Gorgeous.' The Doctor reached out to touch it and the blue light faded to a soft green. 'It's still logged in.'

'What is it?' Amy breathed.

The Doctor looked over and grinned. 'It's a games console.'

'Like an Xbox or a PlayStation?' Rory asked.

'Yeah, if they were able to read and adapt to your thought patterns while stimulating all five senses through manipulating chemicals in your brain.' The Doctor gave him a look.

'I'm sure I saw an advert for something like that,' Rory muttered.

'So this is what's been giving out the energy signal?' asked Amy.

The Doctor pulled the chair out from beneath the desk and perched himself upon it. 'Yep, it's still connected to the network – checking for updates, new software, that kind of thing.'

'But where is it getting the power from?'

The Doctor leant back in his chair and began toying with the wishbone. 'The batteries in these Desktops are immense. They have to be. All the major cities moved their power plants away from populated areas a good century back. There's no such thing as mains power any more. It's all hydrogen batteries now.'

'But how does that –' Rory began, but Amy interrupted him.

'We're missing the big question here. If that thing's still logged on, it means there's still an Internet, or holo-net, or whatever the future-people call it.'

The Doctor frowned. 'Good point.'

'And seeing as everything else is on the blink around here, it seems to me like someone's put some serious effort into making sure it was still working.'

The Doctor tapped the desk; it beeped encouragingly. 'Well,' he said finally, 'I guess I'd better find out what's going on then.' He grabbed the wishbone, and before Amy or Rory could stop him he'd slotted it over his forehead.

'Oh, great,' said Rory.

Seven miles away, sitting in the shadow of a rolling dune, a giant robot was reading a book. The air was still and calm and the robot held the thick paperback at an angle so that the sun's light fell across the pages from over the ridge behind it.

Its metal exoskeleton was heavy and thickset. The erosion of countless sandstorms gave the chrome finish a rugged texture that made it look more animal than machine. From a distance it almost looked like a silver gorilla.

A curved plasma screen stood in place of a face and it traced a blue bead of light to the bottom of the paragraph. Then, with a loud hiss of hydraulics, the robot's arm flexed to turn over the yellowing page.

Then an alarm sounded. The blue bead danced for a minute as a low wail emerged from the speakers fitted in the centre of the robot's chest. Then the screen refreshed and a scrolling message appeared. In square red capitals it repeated the words 'USER DETECTED, USER DETECTED, USER DETECTED,' over and over again.

The robot's shoulders slumped in a digital

sigh. With a great effort and clanging of pistons it hauled itself to its feet and began walking slowly up the side of the dune.

Its great weight caused its feet to slide in the loose sand with each step, but eventually it reached the top. Stretching across the length of the horizon, the half-buried city of Chicago looked like the skeleton of some ancient whale. The robot's screen dimmed as it scanned the ancient buildings for the location of the download.

Eventually a small beep announced that the user had been located. The robot crouched; flexing its steel joints, then launched itself into the air.

CHAPTER 3

TUTORIAL

The Doctor didn't exist.

At least, not yet. Inside the Desktop his mind floated in a void that was made even more confusing by the fact that he didn't have a body. If he had had feet he could at least have found out which direction was 'down'.

Then there were letters.

'Welcome to Parallife,' they said.

The Doctor would've laughed at that if he had a mouth.

'Parallel-life. Very good,' he thought instead.

The letters rearranged themselves. 'Are you a new user?'

'Yes.' The Doctor was getting the hang of thinking instead of speaking now.

'Thank you, please proceed to the Character Creation menu.'

There was a feeling of rapid movement, although in the blackness it was impossible to tell. A light came on, and the Doctor suddenly realised that he was in a room – a huge, white space in which various body parts, clothes and sliding menu-bars were floating. He stepped forward and discovered that he now had a body. Looking down he saw a green wireframe skeleton. He raised a stick figure hand in front of his face and waved at himself.

'Well, I've received a few new bodies in my time, but nothing like this,' he declared, peering around at the vast number of options in front of him. 'This is going to be fun.'

He raised his hands like a conductor preparing to perform and began. Chins, eyes, hair, arms, legs, hands were all selected and adjusted with a wave of the Doctor's hand. They zipped forward and slotted into place over the green skeleton. When he was satisfied, he dismissed the body parts and brought forward the clothes. Boots, skinny trousers, a white shirt. Unfortunately, the only bow tie the Doctor could find was a comically oversized affair.

Finally, he brought up the 'preview' mirror and discovered that he had made a perfect digital replica of himself.

'Well, would you believe it?' he said to himself, rolling up his shirtsleeves. 'And I thought I was just picking what looked cool! You can't improve on perfection, I suppose.'

The Doctor ran a hand over his hair, pushing his long fringe off to one side and dismissed the mirror. He looked up and spread his arms. 'Right, I'm ready!' he said. 'Let's get started!'

There was no reply, but when the Doctor looked forwards once again he found a small red door sitting in the middle of the wall as if it had been there all along. Which it definitely hadn't.

The Doctor did a little hop of excitement. 'Get ready, Parallife,' he said. 'Here I come!'

The town of Tutorial brought back long forgotten memories to Blondie. It was the town of her birth, and like most things she had experienced when she was young, it was far smaller than she remembered. The buildings here were left over from the old world, barely four storeys high and the ground was all on one level. Blondie considered it boring, but if she needed help, this was the best place to find it.

Blondie had never seen so many people in Tutorial before. She suspected that they too had arrived to refresh their training in preparation for fighting the darkness. It had been so long since any of them had fought.

She made her way to the town square, a

large open space where the crowd was at its thickest. She pushed through the mass of people until she was standing in the exact centre of the crowd and drew her sword. She held the shimmering blade high over her head. The weapon was unique and powerful and its very presence created an immediate hush. The crowd stepped back and cleared a circle around her. She opened her mouth to speak, ready to announce that she would lead the fight against the darkness, and that anyone who wished to aid in the defence of their world was welcome to stand by her side. But she didn't get the chance.

The sky above Tutorial cracked, and a digital thunderclap washed over the square. A great column of white light arced down, hitting the ground just half a metre away from where Blondie was standing.

A red door materialised in the glow, and amongst the crowd someone screamed.

'No, it can't be!'

'Impossible!'

'It's been years, so many years!'

But it was true. For the first time in over one hundred years, the world of Parallife had a new citizen.

The door opened and a man stepped out, onto Blondie's foot.

Blondie winced and the man's hand flew instinctively to his oversized bow tie.

'It's a bit large I suppose,' he said. 'But I didn't think it was that bad.' He extended a hand in greeting. 'I'm the Doctor, I'm here to help.'

The crowd held their breath, as if his touch might tear their world apart. But Blondie shook his hand fearlessly and when nothing happened they heaved a sigh of relief.

'Blimey, everyone seems a bit . . . tense.' The Doctor frowned and looked around.

'Parallife is threatened Doctor.' Blondie's

face was grim. 'We must fight or die.'

'Or fight and die.'

'I can see you're going to be a great help.'

The Doctor and Blondie eyed each other with suspicion, until a soft rumble broke the silence. The citizens' eyes rose instinctively to the sky. Another visitor?

But the pink-tinged clouds remained calm, and the rumble continued to grow. On the outskirts of the square, one of the men turned to look down the wide main road behind him. His mouth opened and closed like a fish for a few moments, until he finally found his voice. 'Stampede!' he screamed.

Tutorial was thrown into panic as the citizens rushed for cover among the narrow alleyways between the buildings, fumbling blindly for their weapons. The Doctor spun on his heel, taking it all in.

'What's going on?' he asked.

'The plains around Tutorial are filled with

animals, easy pickings for young citizens to practise their fighting skills. A stampede is the easiest way to level up,' Blondie replied.

'Level up?' the Doctor was incredulous. 'Wait, are you saying that we're in some kind of game?'

'We used to be.' Blondie flexed her sword arm and planted her legs firmly apart. She adopted a fighting stance as the smaller, faster creatures began to pour into the square around them. Three legged birds hopped and skipped across the metal cobbles, their long necks twisting this way and that, searching for a way through. Behind them came the larger mammals. They tumbled through the birds, sending them scattering in all directions.

'They're scared,' the Doctor muttered. 'Terrified.'

There was a loud squawk as one of the creatures picked the wrong alleyway and was struck down by a citizen hidden in a doorway.

It dissolved into a shower of pixels, which flowed into the young warrior, making his skin glow.

'Stop!' the Doctor was outraged. 'You can't do that!' But the citizens ignored him. Growing in confidence, they stepped out of their hiding places and swiped clumsily at the animals as they swept past.

Blondie flashed him a mocking smile. 'Do you really think they'll listen to you? You're level one! Zero experience. You can't hope to command anyone until at least level seven!'

The Doctor looked aghast. 'But I'm a talker, that's what I do, I save people with words, I –'

'It means nothing here,' Blondie interrupted. 'Unless you level-up your negotiation skills, you're powerless. So I suggest you get fighting.'

Even larger animals were beginning to spill through now; huge, buffalo-type creatures whose almost human eyes were wide with fear. Blondie raised her sword, and brought it flashing down.

But it never reached its target. The Doctor's hand snapped out and held firmly onto her wrist as the creature galloped past the pair. Then he twisted her arm up until the sword was pointing away from the steadily growing flood of panicked creatures.

'What are you doing?' she hissed at him, furious. 'We're right in the path of the stampede, if we don't do something we'll be trampled to death!'

'I know,' the Doctor's voice was stern, his grip unwavering. 'What level are you?'

Blondie stared at him.

'What level are you?' the Doctor shouted this time.

'Forty-seven.'

'Good, and from what little chance I've had to look around, it appears that you're the most experienced citizen here.'

Blondie looked smug.

'Which means you should be able to command these people, right?'

'Of course.'

'Then stop the killing!'

CHAPTER 4
LEVEL ZERO

A few minutes later, the Doctor found himself perched on top of Tutorial's town hall. He looked down at the mass of animals that now filled the streets below. It was strange how in this world there was no smell. Blondie had done as he asked and now the citizens were gathered on the surrounding rooftops, away from the peril of the stampede. They eyed the creatures with disappointment as they rumbled through the alleyways beneath.

'Did we fly up here?' the Doctor asked Blondie.

Blondie laughed, a beautiful sound that sparkled like her eyes. 'Of course. Do you not have magic where you come from?' She gestured to the buffalos below. 'They're just programmes you know, they don't even have brains, just a list of things to do. I've never known anyone to care about them before.'

The Doctor was silent for a minute as he absorbed the details of this strange new world.

'Thank you,' he said finally. 'I know that must have been a difficult choice for you to make.'

'It's the rules of the game,' the young woman replied. 'We have to kill or our levels don't rise. If they don't rise we can't create. Our tools, our buildings, our society are founded on the skills we buy with the experience points we gain from battle. There is no other way.'

The Doctor shook his head sadly.

'But in reality, Doctor, the choice wasn't difficult. Because even I can see that it is useless to fight the darkness.' She pointed, and the Doctor followed her gaze.

Tutorial was only a small town. From his position on the roof, the Doctor could see the buildings give way to the plains beyond. Huge, neon-bordered squares marked them out, narrowing as they stretched away to the dark horizon. But something was wrong. The Doctor looked up at the sky. The clouds above shifted on the winds of a distant rhythm, and behind them the sky was still a warm, glowing pink. It was then that the Doctor realised he wasn't looking at the horizon – it was the darkness.

The expanding ebony sphere was now so huge that it no longer looked like a sphere. The curve of its surface was lost against the sky and it looked like a huge, impenetrable wall, bulldozing through the plains towards them.

'Right, well, now I see why the animals were so afraid.'

'They weren't afraid,' Blondie sighed, 'they're simply programmed to avoid danger.'

The Doctor looked at her. 'Isn't that what fear is?'

She smiled. 'Does everything you say make upside-down sense?'

'Not everything. Sometimes I don't make any sense at all.' He swayed slowly to his feet. 'Now, since you're happy to admit that we've no way of fighting this . . . thing. I suggest we follow the animals and get out of here as quickly as possible.'

Blondie took hold of his hand, ready to return them both to the ground. 'We could follow them,' she admitted, a sly grin spreading across her face, 'or we could hitch a ride . . .'

CHAPTER 5
A NEW ARRIVAL

The Doctor had been logged into the computer for over half an hour now. The tiny flat had become cramped and stuffy a long time ago – even with the tiny window open.

It had been Amy's suggestion to climb to the roof and admire the view while they waited, but the lifts had stopped working again and they had to take the stairs. There were seventy floors in total and Rory made sure to remind Amy of that fact as they passed each one.

His feet hurt.

'My feet hurt,' he said for the fifth time.

'Nearly there now.'

'They hurt bad. Like, blisters and things.'

'It'll be worth it when we get to the top.'

Finally they passed the uppermost floor and opened the hot metal door to the roof. A cool breeze washed over them and Rory undid a second button on his shirt. He held his arms away from his sides to fully enjoy the sensation as he walked across the burnt grey paving slabs that wound a path through the broken air-conditioning vents and shattered maintenance boxes.

He put his arm around Amy as they reached the edge and gazed out at the ruins beyond. The view took their breath away.

'It's like . . . everything is sky,' Rory said.

From this height, the blinding heat of the sun appeared to have frozen the desert into glass. The dunes scattered a ragged reflection of the white-blue sky above. Even the nearby buildings were reflected, giving the impression that the entire city was simply –

'Floating. That's what it feels like,' Amy

replied. 'And there's not a cloud in the sky. Do you think there's any water left in the world?'

'I don't know,' said Rory, squinting his eyes against the glare and looking around. 'Although,' he motioned with his hand. 'There's that.'

Amy turned to her right. A single cloud hung on the horizon, a plume of glittering white that seemed to stretch for miles.

'Uh, Rory, I don't think that's a cloud,' she said nervously. 'I think that's a sandstorm.'

'Well it would be, wouldn't it?' Rory had travelled with the Doctor long enough to expect anything less dangerous. 'What shall we do?'

Amy's reply was drowned out by a loud thud. It echoed loudly around the tower block and slowly the pair returned their gaze to the desert.

A large round crater had appeared in the sand, just over a mile away from where the pair were standing.

'There!' Amy pointed to the sky and Rory raised his eyes just in time to see a silver streak falling back down to Earth.

Another thud, another crater. Closer this time.

'What,' said Rory, 'was that?'

They didn't have to wait long to find out.

The object cannoned into the side of the tower block nearly twenty floors below with a crash that made the entire building shudder. Rory stumbled dangerously close to the edge of the roof but Amy grabbed him as she dropped to her knees beside him. Wrapping an arm around his legs for support, she leaned over the ledge and looked down.

Clinging to the side of the structure, covered in grey concrete dust, was a giant robot. As they watched, it turned its smooth, featureless head upwards towards them, and the image of a bright yellow smiley face appeared on its screen. The face winked.

With a loud crunch, the robot withdrew a fist from the wall and smashed it into the floor above to pull itself up. Then it did the same with its other fist. Slowly, the robot began to climb up the tower block, almost demolishing the wall as it did so. Broken glass and bits of plaster exploded outwards with each calculated punch, cascading over the robot's metal back like water.

'Uh,' Rory put a hand on Amy's shoulder. 'Shouldn't we be, um, running? Or something?'

'I don't know. It seems pretty friendly, what with the smiley face and all.'

'Yeah, but maybe that's how it tricks people into letting it kill them. I mean, how do we know it wasn't an army of robots that destroyed the planet in the first place? And demolishing this city isn't just them finishing the job?'

'Could be,' Amy replied. 'But either way, it doesn't exactly look like the kinda thing we could run away from, does it?'

Rory swallowed and winced as the building shuddered from another blow by the robot. 'Well, you're the boss,' he said finally.

So they waited, until eventually the robot's huge metal hand smashed through the ledge of the roof. It hauled its massive bulk onto the paving slabs. The slabs cracked.

'Well you . . . are definitely a lot bigger than I thought,' Rory finished lamely. Cautiously, Amy raised a hand and waggled her fingers in greeting.

'Hi,' she said.

The robot looked at them.

'Hello.' Its voice crackled slightly, and it looked down to see that its speaker was clogged with dust. There was a sudden burst of noise, and a small grey cloud burst from its chest. When it spoke again its voice was far deeper than before. 'Let's try that again: hello? Hello.'

'Did that robot just clear its throat at us?' whispered Amy.

'I think it just did,' Rory replied.

The robot ignored them. 'I'm sorry to bother you,' it continued, 'but I'm afraid an army of robots is heading this way and they're programmed to demolish the city.'

There was silence for a moment, then Rory folded his arms and turned to face his wife. 'This,' he said triumphantly, gesturing at the robot behind him with his thumb, 'is why you should always listen to me.'

CHAPTER 6
DEMOLITION

A short while later, Amy and Rory had led the robot down into the hallway outside apartment 23B. Its huge frame left long scratches down each side of the corridor and with every shuddering step, Rory had visions of them all plummeting down to ground level.

'So, what do we call you?' Amy asked the robot. 'Do you have a name?'

'My name is Daryl,' the robot replied.

Rory sniggered and Daryl's smiley face transformed into a frown. Rory stopped sniggering immediately. 'Nice to meet you, Daryl,' he said.

The door opposite the Doctor's apartment

had been left ajar. Now it swung backwards and forwards in a heavy breeze, beating a regular rhythm against the frame.

'That's funny,' said Amy. She stepped forward to prevent another slam, 'I can't remember it being this windy when we arrived.'

She looked out through the broken hole in the side of the tower block. The sandstorm was larger now, much larger.

'They're coming,' said Daryl

'Wait, you mean that sandstorm is the robot army you warned us about?'

Daryl nodded.

Rory swallowed. 'How many of them are there?'

'It takes 347 to span the length of a city this large.'

'But what's the point? There aren't any humans left to enslave!'

'Enslave?' Daryl's screen refreshed and a large blue question mark appeared. 'They're helping humanity. And even if they could think for themselves, what would they need with human slaves?'

'Well, in the movies . . .' Rory trailed off.

Daryl shook his head in disbelief.

'But why would humanity want their world demolished?' Amy stepped in.

'Demolition is only the first stage. They're preparing the ground to rebuild the planet.'

'So unless we grab the Doctor and get out of here sharpish we'll become the foundations for Chicago 2. I get it, right, let's go!' She pushed open the door to apartment 23B, and strode over to where the Doctor was still sitting, slumped in his chair and connected to the Desktop.

'Wait, don't –' she heard Rory call over her shoulder, before he was drowned out by an almighty crash.

Amy turned to see Daryl standing in the

doorway. Or at least where the doorway used to be. The wooden frame was now perched at an angle across Daryl's back and behind him the plaster of the wall had been smashed through in a perfect outline of the robot.

'— do that.' Rory finished quietly, standing on tiptoe to look over Daryl's shoulder and into the room.

Daryl raised a finger and pointed at the Desktop. A small shower of plaster powder tumbled to the floor as he did so. 'Do not unplug the user,' he said.

'What? Why?' Amy's hand hovered over the small green power light.

'It's dangerous.'

'More dangerous than getting demolished by an army of robot-bulldozers?'

'That is unfair.'

Amy rolled her eyes and moved to press the Desktop. In a flurry of movement, Daryl's arm snapped out. It extended on a piston and grabbed her by the shoulder, pulling her away from the desk.

Amy squealed, more out of surprise than anything else. Daryl's grip was surprisingly gentle.

'Hey! Hands off my missus!' Rory banged on one of Daryl's shoulder blades with a fist.

'If he is unplugged before he logs out, his mind will be separated from his body and his body will short-circuit.' To illustrate his point, Daryl's face flashed up a smiley face with crosses for eyes.

'Ouch,' muttered Amy. 'Then how does he get out?'

'He needs to find a save-point. It will store his online character and return his mind to his real-world body.'

'But he doesn't know that he needs to save!'

'I am connected to the network – if he hasn't moved far from the Tutorial zone I may be able to save him externally.' Moving

Amy carefully aside, Daryl spread his right hand over the Desktop. From the inside of his palm, mini-pistons began to drop down and connect with the surface. The Desktop rippled with light as the pistons began to tap on its surface. It looked as if the finish was being struck by neon-water droplets. Amy thought it was beautiful.

'Amy, I think you'd better look at this.' Rory's voice broke her concentration. She rushed over to where he was standing in the hallway, looking out at the approaching sandstorm.

It was much closer now, and through the rippling grains of glass sand, the pair could begin to make out the large, dark outlines of the demolition robots. They were huge.

'We're running out of time,' Rory hissed urgently and, as if in response, the edge of the storm smashed into one of the outer buildings of the city.

There was a terrible, crunching grinding noise, like nails scraping across a blackboard, only a thousand times louder.

Amy covered her ears with her hands as the building began to shake.

'Daryl! Tell me you're done!' she shouted over the din.

Daryl straightened up, and turned his screen towards them. On it was a sad face.

'The user has left the area. I am unable to pull him out.'

'The Doctor! He's called the Doctor!' Amy ran over to him and flung her arms up in frustration. 'There's got to be something, he'll do something, that's what he does, escapes in the nick of time and –'

The tower block shuddered again, longer and louder this time as another building was chewed up by the advancing bulldozers.

'The nick of time has just run out,' Daryl

stated. 'We have to go.'

'No! We're not leaving him!' Rory was in the doorway now, his head and shoulders white with plaster dust. 'You're a robot! Call them off!'

Daryl shook his head. 'I am not . . . operating within my programming. They will not listen to me and I can't risk my actions being discovered.'

Amy and Rory exchanged puzzled glances.

'What?'

'What?!'

Daryl waved them into silence, demolishing half the bathroom in the process. 'I do, however, have this.' A small hatch popped open in his thigh and he produced a small white sphere that immediately sprouted four legs. He reached down and placed it carefully on the floor beneath the Doctor's chair. 'An emergency beacon. It forbids the bulldozers to demolish anything within two metres square of its location.'

They looked at the device doubtfully. It blinked at them. Then, before they could protest, Daryl reached out two massive hands and grabbed them both. Holding them tightly to his chest, he bent his knees with a sharp hiss of hydraulics.

'Hopefully,' he finished, before jumping through the wall.

Daryl set Amy and Rory down two miles away on the opposite side of the city. They staggered to their feet, battered and bruised, and turned to watch as the sandstorm swamped the tower block they had been standing in only a few minutes before. The wall of sand dwarfed even the tallest skyscrapers, and they looked on in horror as each one was transformed into a shower of glittering dust.

Rory put a hand on Amy's arm, but he had no words to comfort her. Soon the city was lost from view.

Amy turned to Daryl and looked at him with hollow eyes.

'What now?' she asked.

In response, Daryl turned away from her and crouched. Then beckoned for them to climb onto his back.

'Now,' he said, 'we run.'

CHAPTER 7
THE FOREST

'**D**o you think your mount could stop trying to eat mine for just five minutes?' the Doctor sniffed. He was perched awkwardly on the back of a small, ostrich-type bird. It waddled under his weight and kept scooting off in the wrong direction whenever he wasn't concentrating.

Blondie was riding a two-metre long tiger. Which was blue.

She had found it prowling around at the edge of the stampede, ready to pick off any stragglers. With a few well-chosen swipes of her sword she had persuaded it to stand still long enough for her to climb onto its back.

Once she had done that, the creature was stuck with her.

It snapped its jaws at the Doctor's ostrich once again and let out a frustrated growl. The noise sent the bird and its rider zigzagging off to hide behind an emerald-coloured tree.

Cautiously, the ostrich poked its head out from behind the trunk and squawked angrily at the tiger. The Doctor's head popped out soon after.

'I suppose this is because I'm a level one animal-trainer-rider type-thing, right?'

Blondie nodded. 'You're getting the hang of it now.'

'And I presume you're on level three trillion and four or something because you're Little Miss Perfect?'

'Well, thirty-five at animal training.'

The ostrich stretched out a bony leg to step cautiously out from behind the tree. The tiger growled and the bird quickly returned to its hiding place.

'Well, if you're so good, how come you can't stop your tiger-thing from trying to eat my chicken-thing?'

'I can. But it's funnier this way.'

'Oh, you are a great help,' the Doctor let out a bitter laugh. 'It's the end of your world and all you can think about is making me look stupid.'

Blondie smiled. 'I've always said it'd be nice to die laughing.' She yanked at the lump of fur behind the tiger's neck that she was using as a rein and reared it away from the bird. 'But obviously your sense of humour is only at level one as well.'

Finally the Doctor was able to control his ride, and trotted out to rejoin Blondie. 'So even a person's sense of humour has a level here?' he asked.

'No, that was a joke.'

'I'll shut up now.'

'Please do.'

They rode on slowly in silence, giving their mounts a chance to rest after the desperate sprint away from Tutorial. The Doctor's mood saddened as he remembered their panicked dash through the stampeding herd. The cries of the citizens and animals still rang in his ears before the digital sounds that made up their voices were disintegrated into megabytes, then kilobytes, then bytes by the relentless advance of the darkness behind them.

But the Doctor and Blondie had stayed ahead of the pack, encouraging their mounts to even greater speeds. Eventually the rumble of destruction faded, and the tidal wave of wreckage was nothing more than a shimmering blur on the horizon behind them.

The Doctor ran a hand through his hair, frustrated. When he looked over to Blondie he realised that she was shaking, but whether it was with anger or fear he couldn't tell. They kept on moving.

Around them colourful branches began to spring from the ground, multiplying and blossoming into the flat outlines of trees. They stretched higher, twisting and turning until the pair were dwarfed by a cool pastel forest. Soon they made their way through the paths between puddles of blue light that flowed from the surrounding roots. The Doctor blinked, attempting to adjust his eyes to the mind-bending structure of the world. He didn't even know whether the sudden appearance of the forest was a trick of the horizon, or if it was truly growing around them.

Blondie spotted his puzzlement. 'It's called pop-in,' she explained. 'This forest has been programmed to exist here, but when there are no citizens around, the network hides it to save memory. We were running so fast earlier that it was having trouble restoring the trees around us, which is why they seem to grow.

Actually, this forest has been here for over fifty years.'

The Doctor gently guided his ostrich over towards the nearest trunk. It was flat and golden, and when he pressed his hand against it, it crackled gently. His palms tingled.

'If a tree falls in a forest, and there's no one around to hear it, does the forest even exist?' he murmured. 'Fascinating.'

Blondie laughed. 'Yeah, I forget just how much Parallife must have changed from your world since the players left.'

The Doctor frowned. 'And how do you know? You're a part of the network, you've never seen the outside world.'

'No, but I was a player's character once, we all were.'

The Doctor stopped and looked at her.

'Do you know what humans do when they're given a blank canvas in virtual reality? When they get the chance to create a new face and a new body from scratch? They make themselves. And then they go out and make their house, and the streets outside their house, and the sky blue and the trees green. Because humans think that it's a skill to make things realistic.' She paused and took a breath. 'What did you look like on the outside?'

The Doctor looked embarrassed. 'Well, kinda like . . . this.'

'Exactly.'

'So all this, Parallife, is an online computer game – where people create their own characters and go on quests and fight monsters and level up and buy shiny swords?' the Doctor said.

'It was an online game. And it used to look like the outside world. Although back then the outside world was called the real world.'

'So what happened?'

'The humans all left. We don't know why.'

The Doctor rubbed his chin.

'Parallife was left empty; all those players' characters just stored online doing nothing,' Blondie said.

'And you, your body and levels and things, you used to be a character? Someone used to play as you?'

Blondie blushed. 'It sounds weird when you put it like that.'

The Doctor looked up towards the sky that tinged the topmost branches of the trees a golden pink. 'I guess that also means there used to be a human that looked like you. Once.'

'I guess so.'

'Weird isn't it? Waking up in a body that isn't yours.' He looked at her sadly for a moment, then looked away. 'Hang on a minute . . .'

'What?' Blondie shook her head to clear her thoughts. She watched as the Doctor jumped easily from the back of the bird and ran over to one of the trees. It was set back from the path they had been travelling on. Had they not stopped there to talk, he may not even have noticed it.

Something was terribly wrong with the tree.

He knelt down, put his hands against the trunk and pushed his face closer to inspect the damage. The tree had a slash across it, half a metre above the ground, which seemed to run right through it. Above and below the slash the trunk was still coloured with a golden haze. But inside there was only an empty blackness – a slice of nothingness that seemed to ooze from the digital bark. It was dripping something softly onto the forest floor, and the Doctor struggled to work out what it was.

Then he realised. The tree was bleeding numbers.

'What is it?' Blondie appeared by his side.

'I hope you made sure your tiger wasn't able to reach my bird.' the Doctor said. He looked over his shoulder to make sure. 'I said –'

'Shut up, Doctor,' said Blondie.

The Doctor turned to look at her. She straightened up, backing slowly away from the tree.

'I think we should get out of here,' she said. And it was then that the Doctor realised she was afraid. Very, very afraid.

'What's going on? What are these numbers?' He reached down to scoop up a handful from the pool on the floor.

When Blondie spoke again, her voice was shaking. 'Nothing, waste data. Something has erased the computer program that makes up the tree so that all that's left is useless code. Lengths, colours, sizes, shapes – now they're all just meaningless numbers.'

'And what can do that?' the Doctor's voice was stern.

'Nothing can do that!'

'Something can!' the Doctor shouted back. 'And you know what it is because otherwise you wouldn't be so scared!'

'I've never seen one,' Blondie shook her head and continued to back away. 'No one's seen one. Sometimes you can hear them.'

'Them?'

'The Defrags!'

'And what,' said the Doctor, 'exactly, is a Defrag?'

'Listen!' Blondie held up a hand.

They stopped and listened, but all the Doctor could hear was the rustling of the trees. Then it hit him. There was no wind. And even if there was, would these trees rustle?

The noise grew louder, becoming a harsh scratching hiss that sounded like radio static with the volume turned up to maximum.

'They're coming,' said Blondie.

CHAPTER 8
DEFRAG

The Doctor and Blondie raced back to the path. They dragged each other over sprouting tree roots and through neon puddles in their haste. The noise was so loud now that they had to cover their ears. Stumbling back onto the path, Blondie hurried to untie her tiger, but the Doctor's ostrich had wandered off. He whistled, sweeping his head from side to side in an attempt to spot it.

'Why didn't you tie it up?' Blondie shouted to him over the noise.

There was a soft pop, a squawk and the Doctor turned slowly back towards Blondie, who was already on her tiger.

'It's gone,' she said. 'We need to go!'

The Doctor made to run, but stopped, suddenly confused. The path ahead and behind them was so filled with shadow that it was difficult to tell which direction they had come from. 'It's too dark to see anything!' he shouted.

'They are the dark,' she said. 'The only things to survive the destruction.'

There was a burst of movement behind him, and the Doctor spun around. The shadows were swarming towards them through the trees now, but they were like no shadow the Doctor had ever seen. As they moved, an outline of corrupted orange data spilled onto the floor around them.

But there was something else as well. The Doctor squinted, fascinated, his eyes desperately trying to penetrate the dark. It almost killed him.

The static noise transformed into a scream

as one of the Defrags plummeted down towards the Doctor from its perch in a decaying tree. He raised his hands to cover his head.

But the impact didn't come. There was a thud and the creature seemed to roll away from the Doctor mid-fall, coming to rest only a couple of metres away on the forest floor. An eerie quiet descended and the noise of the Defrags was softened. The Doctor could hear running water.

'Did you see that?' the Doctor turned to his companion. 'It's like some kind of force . . .' His voice trailed off. 'Field.'

From her position on the tiger, Blondie had raised her palm to the sky. From it, a fountain of white energy was pouring upwards. It hung in the air for a moment, transforming into water before arcing down around them in a perfect circle. It was this that the Defrag had hit.

'It's a water sphere,' she said, 'I designed it myself.'

The Doctor said nothing. He stepped over to the edge of the circle where the Defrags were gathering and pressed his face against the water-screen.

A shattered face looked back. Like a reflection in a broken mirror.

'There's something inside the shadows,' the Doctor breathed. 'Something broken.'

In response, a curling red claw reached out to prod at the opposite side of the shield. The Doctor recognised parts of the creature as human, or animal, but the jumbled mess that made up the whole was horrific and unnatural.

The creature howled in frustration. It began beating its face and claws against the water in a terrible drumbeat. The rest of the Defrags took up its rhythm until the water dome's surface became a mess of shuddering ripples.

'Doctor, I can't sustain this spell forever!' Blondie called over to him.

'Quiet!' said the Doctor. 'I'm thinking.'

He got to his feet and began to pace around the protected circle, meeting the gaze of each Defrag as he did so.

'When did you make this spell?' he gestured to Blondie's palm. 'After the humans left?'

Blondie nodded.

'Right, and these trees, they're not realistic, but they're still based on the human programming of a tree, with the colours and textures changed?'

'Most things in this world are.'

'So people have been taking the human-made outfits and features and expanding them to create new objects. Could they create new faces? New clothes and hands and other things I haven't got time to think of?'

'For the right price. Only a few citizens have a level high enough to do such complex work. They must pay to have their designs created by the Guild of Architects.'

'That's it!' the Doctor declared triumphantly.

He pointed at the snarling face of the nearest Defrag with both hands. 'That's what these are, and that's what the blackness is!'

'What?' Blondie's arm was shaking now. Sweat glistened on her face, and the white stream of energy pouring through her was beginning to grey.

'It's a system wipe. Something is trying to erase all the data on the network.'

'But that's our world!'

'Of course it is. But this thing doesn't know that, it thinks Parallife is empty, that nothing happened once the humans left. But things did happen, you created new things; new people and places and the system can't tell that. It's only erasing the programs created by humanity, not yours.'

Blondie's eyes widened. 'Which means that –'

'The Defrags are what's left of people like you! They're what's left when the human designs of your bodies are erased, only your new clothes and faces and stuff are left. They're upgrades held together by shadow.'

'But what's left is still affected by new programmes like mine?'

'Exactly.'

Blondie's sleeve was beginning to blacken now as the shield began to stutter. Around them the Defrags were beginning to sense the weakening in the water shield, and their screams of frustration transformed into gloating howls.

'Now we can go!' the Doctor grinned, running over to sit behind her on the tiger's back.

'Oh, no, you don't!' Blondie grinned. 'You can't just reveal that there's a way to fight these things and then expect me to run.'

The Doctor's face fell. 'They're not your enemy, Blondie, fighting them isn't going to help!'

'They're monsters, Doctor, they've haunted my city, my home and my life. I'm tired of being scared.' She clicked her fingers and the water shield evaporated into a cloud of steam. Then she drew her sword.

The blade flashed in the shadows, reflecting rainbows off the cloud as the water settled into a thick mist. It flowed between the decaying trees, covering the forest floor. The Defrags remained hidden in the steam, but the hiss of static made ripples in the mist.

Blondie's silver eyes narrowed as she encouraged the tiger into motion. She swept the blade from side to side through the steam, smiling as it crackled on contact with the water droplets. The Doctor, clinging tightly to her waist, eyed her carefully. There was obviously no reasoning with her like this.

'This sword is one of the most complex programmes the Chief Architect has ever created. A one hit kill. Now I have an enemy that deserves such a weapon.'

The mist stirred around them, and exploded into life.

The Defrags leapt high into the air, water streaming through the shadows of their bodies. Blondie smiled and began to spin the blade in her hand faster and faster, whipping up the air around them as she prepared to strike the monsters.

It was only then that she realised they were leaping in the opposite direction, away from her. A few moments later the forest was silent once more, and the Defrags had fled.

Blondie let out a yell of anger, and slashed at the ground with her sword. 'How dare you?' she called out at the empty trees. 'How dare you run from me?'

The Doctor put a comforting hand on Blondie's shoulder. 'They're scared.'

'They've no right to be scared!'

The Doctor said nothing. Instead he spurred the tiger into motion, and together they rode on towards the edge of the forest.

CHAPTER 9
THE OTHER SIDE

Eventually the trees opened out onto the edge of a huge cliff, and the tiger refused to go any further. The Doctor and Blondie dismounted and looked out at a haze of sky.

'It feels like the edge of the world,' he said.

Blondie looked at him. 'We can't run forever.'

'I know. But those Defrags, Blondie, they're not the monsters. Inside each shattered body is the mind of a citizen. They're trapped. Of all the things that have been added to this world since the players left, their minds – your mind – are the only things that are completely new. They are the only things that cannot be harmed by the system wipe. One of your friends could be inside one of those creatures – unable to speak. How would you feel if your touch could infect the foundations of Parallife?'

Blondie looked away. 'You're right, of course, but what will become of them? Of us? Will we end up trapped inside a world of nothing?'

'I don't know.'

'The Games Master would know.'

The Doctor raised an eyebrow.

'The Games Master is our creator. He used to monitor Parallife when the humans were still players. It was his job to create new quests, missions and battles to be fought. When the players left, he gave each of their characters a mind of their own. We only exist because of him,' Blondie explained.

'And where is he now?'

'Gone.'

'Where?'

'Who knows?'

She reached up to her sleeve and fingered the burnt material from where she had cast her spell. 'Maybe he thought we weren't good enough and created the darkness –'

'The system wipe.'

'Whatever – to correct his mistake.' Blondie tore off her tattered sleeve and held it out over the cliff. She watched the wind tug at it for a moment then let go. The cloth fluttered for a moment then seemed to fall towards the cliff-face, sticking to the side.

The Doctor looked down.

'Wow,' he said finally.

The cliff face stretched away below them, as far as the eye could see, and on it a spiralling twisting architecture soared into the sky. Cities and homes and villages, some on a level, some at right angles, some whose internal pathways seemed to fold and loop impossibly around each other.

And it glowed, all of it, a blossoming firework frozen in time.

'We're not on the edge of the world at all, are we?' the Doctor said eventually, 'We're on the side of it.'

Blondie laughed. 'Your mind is too practical, Doctor. What's up and down are not constant here; the Architects change them as they like.'

'The Architects!' The Doctor slapped his forehead. 'That's where we need to go. Take me there.'

'I was going to,' Blondie said.

She took his hand, and together they stepped onto the top of the world.

CHAPTER 10
SAFETY

Vast sand dunes swept by beneath Daryl's feet. Miles and miles of rippling desert that seemed to stretch across the entire world, and probably did for all Amy and Rory knew.

They clung on tightly to his curved metal shoulder blades. Each time the robot landed they were thrown high into the air with the force of the impact, before he launched himself away again. And each time he reached the peak of his impossible leap they experienced a feeling of weightlessness. They hung in the air as if gravity was still struggling to catch up with them, before plummeting down to Earth with a turn of their stomachs.

Amy's legs and arms now ached so much that she could barely feel them, and her hair had been blown into a tangled mess by the speed of Daryl's travel. She looked over to Rory, but his eyes were fixed firmly on his sweaty palms, as if willing them to keep holding on. Once he looked over Daryl's shoulder and saw the ground hurtling away beneath them. He almost fainted.

'You weren't scared when we went on that death mountain ride at Alton Towers,' Amy shouted over the wind.

'That had a height restriction and a safety bar!'

Daryl's body hit the ground once more, sending up a spray of sand. Amy screwed shut her eyes, coughing and spitting the sand from her mouth. When she opened them again, Rory had gone, and beneath her Daryl was standing motionless at the top of a dune.

With a long groan of pain, Amy prised

her fingers away from their handhold and slid slowly down Daryl's back onto the hot sand. She lay there for a moment, willing her muscles to unlock, then wobbled to her feet, legs slipping everywhere.

'This is gonna hurt in the morning,' she said, attempting to shake some life into her limbs.

Finally confident that she could walk, she turned to look down the side of the dune behind her. She followed the long trail of upturned sand that zigzagged away from her. Then her eyes rested upon the dazed figure of Rory, lying face down in the valley of the dune.

She slipped and slid her way down the loose sand, accidentally spraying him as she dropped to her knees by his side.

'Blegh,' said Rory, his face muffled by the sand.

'You okay?'

'Blegh.'

Amy sighed. 'I'll take that as a "yes."'

Rory tried to roll over and groaned. 'My arms and legs have stopped working.'

'They just ache, get up!' She grabbed his arm and hauled Rory to his feet, ignoring his half-hearted protests.

'I don't like the future any more. Can we go to the past next time?'

'If you're good.'

She dusted him down and together they turned to see Daryl still waiting for them at the top of the dune. Then they began the long climb up to meet him.

'It's shady on the other side, we'll stop for a rest.' Amy promised.

'There's no need for that.' Daryl said, as they hauled themselves onto the ridge. 'We're here.'

An arrow flashed up on his face and Amy and Rory looked across the other side of the dune.

The sun was hanging lower in the sky now, and the once flawless white sea of sand was now patterned with lengthening shadows that turned the landscape a stark black and white. At the base of the dune was a bunker, its metal outline shining where it caught the sun above the shadow.

Two huge double doors faced them, and the ribbed girders that lined the building's roof were rusted a sunburnt orange. Surrounded by the wildness of the landscape, its solid angles looked strangely out of place. It looked like a stranded ship, or a skyscraper on its side.

'What is it?' asked Amy.

Daryl shifted; sand pouring from the cracks in his metal skeleton as he prepared to move again.

'Safety,' he said.

CHAPTER 11
THE BUNKER

The interior of the bunker was vast and still, bathed in a shadow that hadn't been disturbed for over a century. Until now.

The giant steel gears that arced around the twenty-storey high double doors began to shake and creak. They rotated agonisingly slowly with a howl of metal grinding on metal. Gradually the doors began to part, and a tiny sliver of light slashed across the floor of the bunker. The column of light grew wider as the grinding squeal increased. Soon, the dark outline of Daryl's silhouette was framed in the crack between the doors. His metal body was dwarfed by the size of the machinery around the doors, but his strength was many times his size. Eventually the double doors were prised open wide enough to allow Amy, Rory and Daryl to step through comfortably.

Amy walked slowly along the path created by the column of light, her footsteps echoing loudly in the gloom. Her eyes widened in the darkness as her sight adjusted to the sudden change, and her mouth opened in awe.

All around her, hanging from the arches of the distant roof, were robots. Each one was the size of a small bus, and their rounded metal joints and steaming hydraulics gave them the appearance of a herd of sleeping dragons. They swung lazily back and forth on their chains, while a network of walkways and control panels threaded between each one. Amy suddenly felt very small.

'It's like a cathedral.' Even Rory's whisper echoed as he walked slowly across to join Amy. 'A cathedral for worshipping giant robots,' he added, looking around.

'Looks like you're the runt of the litter, Daryl,' Amy called over her shoulder.

'We aren't related.' Daryl strode over to them with a great deal of noise, his footsteps ringing on the metal floor.

Rory shivered, it was cold inside the bunker. A welcome relief from the sweltering sun outside. 'I thought you were taking us to safety?' he asked. 'I presumed that would mean as far away from an army of robots as possible.'

'This is the safest place on the planet.' The smiling face returned to Daryl's screen.

'How?'

'The rebuilding of Earth is a two-stage process. Demolition followed by reconstruction. Outside, the planet is being flattened and processed, prepared for the second stage.'

'And these are the reconstruction robots?' Amy stepped cautiously across the room to stand beneath one of the giants. A huge, blank plasma screen stared back, surrounded by a cluster of cylinders.

'Correct. There are five hundred of these factories positioned across the globe, each one containing an army of similar size. These bunkers are the only places Legacy has been programmed not to demolish.'

'Well, duh,' said Rory. 'Be a pretty stupid plan otherwise.'

'Legacy?' Amy held a finger to Rory's mouth and encouraged Daryl to continue.

'Legacy is the Central Intelligence, it controls all artificial life on the planet – coordinating the restoration of Earth.'

'Including you?'

'I am . . .' Daryl paused. 'Unique.'

'Is that a no?'

'Yes.'

'Yes, that's a no or yes, Legacy controls you?'

'Legacy doesn't control me.'

Rory put his head in his hands. The sun had given him a headache. 'Hang on a minute.' He screwed his face up, trying to think. 'Why?' he finished.

'Why what?' Daryl flashed a question mark.

'Why the whole "restoration" thing? There isn't anybody left to appreciate this whole . . .' he flapped his hand around, 'whatever it is.'

Daryl raised his screen upwards, running a blue bead across the surfaces of the suspended robots. It flashed across their chrome surfaces, disappearing into the darkness above each one before reappearing on the next. As he did so, each robot jerked into life for an instant. The cylinders around their screen-faces slid open to reveal an array of mechanical arms, each especially constructed for a different purpose. The motors in their bodies flexed and twitched with a series of loud hisses before the blue dot continued on and left its target swinging slowly from its chains, dormant once more.

'There's you,' he said finally.

Amy and Rory stared at each other.

'Us?'

Daryl shrugged, a gesture that seemed strange and unnatural when performed by an artificial body.

Rory stepped forward. 'You're trying to say that all of this, this . . . Legacy stuff is to give us somewhere to live? You're trying to rebuild a planet for two human beings?'

'I had expected a greater number of survivors.' Daryl's smiley face flipped into a frown.

'Maybe they're all in other bunkers,' Amy suggested.

Daryl shook his head. 'The bunkers are empty except for the robots.'

Rory laughed. 'Yeah and you went round the entire planet to check did you?'

Daryl was silent,

'Oh my God. You did!'

'I had one hundred years.'

In that moment Amy felt a pang of sympathy for Daryl. She reached out a hand and gently touched it against Daryl's forearm.

'I'd nearly given up.' He continued, 'And then the demolition army was activated. But I found you in the end.'

'You must have been lonely.'

'I had a book.'

Rory whistled through his teeth. 'Well, I hope we were worth the effort.'

Daryl's yellow face winked at them. 'To be honest I thought you'd be taller. Or stronger; more like me. I was surprised to find that you humans are so . . . fragile.'

'He's never seen a human before!' Rory hissed.

'So?'

'Shhh!' He looked nervously around. It had been nearly half an hour since their conversation with Daryl. With nothing left to do but wait, the robot had produced his book from a hidden compartment in his stomach and settled himself in the middle of the bunker to read. Rory had taken this opportunity to guide Amy away, up the network of stairways and gantries into the highest, furthest corner they could reach.

They huddled behind the bulk of one of the reconstruction robots, unable to see each other in the gloom that surrounded them. But Rory was still scared.

'Don't you see what that means?' he whispered once more.

He felt, rather than saw, Amy shake her head.

'It means we can't trust him. Haven't you been listening to anything Daryl's said? He's got no idea what's going on with the Legacy thing, he obviously wasn't built by a human, and he's rather keen to keep his actions on the down-low.'

'The down-low?' Amy giggled.

'Having one lone robot jumping around the planet, looking for the last surviving humans just doesn't fit with a plan to rebuild Earth. If the human race had the intelligence to put Legacy in motion, then it should have had the intelligence to keep itself alive during the end of the world or whatever.'

'So where do you think he came from?' Amy asked.

Rory shrugged. 'I dunno. He's obviously more alive than the others.'

Amy said nothing.

Rory continued, 'So what're we gonna do? Make a run for it?'

'He saved our lives!' Amy said. 'If we leave now we'll be shredded by the demolition robots.'

'But . . . why did he save our lives?'

'I don't know!' Amy was becoming more and more frustrated. 'Why don't we just ask him?'

Rory inched over to the railings at the edge of the gantry and looked down at where Daryl was sitting, a dizzying distance below.

Something was wrong.

The robot's book was lying on the floor a short distance from where he was sitting. Although Rory couldn't see his face, the pulsing red glow that illuminated Daryl's arms and legs could only be coming from one place.

Cautiously, Rory stood up and softly padded along the gantry to try and get a view of Daryl's screen. Amy clattered after him in her boots.

'Can you hear that?' she whispered.

'Yeah, how about you start wearing trainers next time we leave the TARDIS?'

'No, no, not that. Listen!'

Rory pricked up his ears.

At this distance the noise was faint. But as he listened, Rory was sure he could hear the sound of a telephone ringing.

CHAPTER 12
NEW PLACES

This side of Parallife was very different to the one they had been on before. The hand of the Architects could be seen wherever the Doctor and Blondie looked. Little remained of the old world. Even the more familiar buildings and people had been restyled almost beyond recognition. Vast, twisting glass landscapes stretched in all directions, and even in the smaller settlements the homes and other constructions were floating in the air, attached to the layered surface by neon strands.

But it was the music that stood out most to the Doctor. Instead of the realistic sound samples of the forest, where rustling leaves and distant birdsong had been the only soundtrack to their journey – here even their footsteps produced soft, musical notes. When the buildings swayed, it was in time to a soft bass rhythm rather than the sound of any wind. The citizens that lived here had hidden their human features beneath rippling pixel-suits that faded from colour to colour in time to the beat. The colours displayed their emotions in a way that made language almost unnecessary. Everything was transmitting information, and for the Doctor – who was used to not judging by appearances – the honesty of the notes and colours was astonishing.

'They make me look almost human, don't they?' Blondie commented to him. And it was true. Before, her silver hair and artificial clothing had stood out amongst the realistic outfits in Tutorial, and the flawless texture of her skin was at odds with the rough, matted fur of the animals they had ridden. Here she was the most familiar sight that the Doctor could see.

'Everything is so open. No one, nothing, has anything to hide. And they couldn't hide it if they wanted to,' he said.

'And what would they want to hide? How could hiding what they feel help a person to be happy?'

They had reached the nearest settlement by now. It was only a small cluster of buildings. The Doctor would have called it a village if the word didn't seem so ridiculous here. They leapt up its levels, to a network of roads that blossomed from the centre of the houses and arced upwards into the sky.

Blondie conjured a guiding spell. She created a small ball of light in her hand and threw it up above their heads. It hovered there for a minute until Blondie spoke, loudly and clearly. 'The Architects' Guild, please.' Then it zipped off towards the horizon. It left a frozen streak of lightning behind it that followed one of the larger roads from the village.

The road was transparent and almost invisible when the pair moved to step onto it. But as they did so, their shadows seemed to become solid beneath them, creating a platform for them to stand on. The Doctor wobbled uncertainly for a moment, and Blondie grabbed his arm to steady him as their shadows began to move.

They raced across the landscape, their path joining a highway a few miles ahead. Around them the world twisted and looped, although the Doctor couldn't be sure if it was the world turning or the highway.

'How far now?' the Doctor shouted, before realising that there was no wind anymore to drown out his words. 'I mean, how far now?' he said again, more quietly. He checked his watch. 'We might have outrun the system wipe so far, but soon there'll be nowhere to run to.'

'If new code is the only protection against the darkness, then the Guild is our last hope for survival,' Blondie replied.

CHAPTER 13
THE GUILD

The Architects' Guild was huge. Great emerald spires seemed to touch the sky and turned the light around it to a deep green that swathed the landscape in a dusky glow. Its shape stretched downwards just as far, its lowest spire connecting to the shimmering grid of the city below. It looked huge. But only after another fifteen minutes of travel, with the spires looming bigger and bigger on the horizon, did the Doctor realise just how huge it really was.

The highway ended in the exact centre of the structure, at its widest point. The Doctor and Blondie stepped out onto a wide glass rim that circled the Guild and attached to a large number of other roads and walkways.

The Doctor knelt down to stare at the city below, touching his hand against the glass. The outlines of its grids and streets, buildings and vehicles, shone brightly in the darkness of the deep green sky.

'Interesting,' said the Doctor.

'What is?' Blondie leaned down beside him.

'Probably nothing.' He leapt to his feet. 'But worth remembering.'

The Doctor strode over to one of the main entrances to the Guild, where two men were standing either side. He smoothed over his hair with a hand and fiddled with his shirt. He fastened the cuffs with ease and straightened his bow tie. Finally, once he considered himself presentable, he offered a hand to one of the men.

'Hello, I'm the Doctor,' he grinned. 'Now if you'd just let me through to see your Chief

Architect, then I might be able to save your world from total destruction.'

The men looked at each other, then back to the Doctor.

'Well, don't tell us,' said one.

'Just walk right in and do it. We aren't going to stop you,' said the other.

The Doctor looked confused. 'But, you're guards aren't you?'

'Guards?!' One of the men looked at him as if he were mad. 'What would anyone need a guard for?'

Blondie strode past the Doctor and through the doors, pretending she wasn't with him.

The Doctor shifted his weight from foot to foot, embarrassed, then hurried in after her.

'For a man so obsessed with peaceful solutions, you expect an awful lot of violence don't you?'

'I just thought, you know.'

'I don't know. Players don't kill players,

what kind of world do you think we live in?'

The Doctor was silent.

The main hall stretched away before them. It was filled with columns that curved out of the floor and extended both above and below the glass floor into the furthest reaches of the Guild. A menu appeared in the air before Blondie with a collection of small, flat rectangles of varying colours. Each one was labelled with a department and room number. She jabbed a finger at a small white box and another lightning streak zipped across the floor and up one of the columns.

'This way,' she said, striding forward.

They walked up the curve of the floor until they were at right angles to where they had just been standing, then carried on upwards.

The Doctor ducked to avoid bumping heads with a citizen walking upside down on a nearby column. As they walked, the building narrowed and the spires split off in all directions.

Eventually their spire was all that was left, and the tunnel that surrounded them drew so close that the Doctor had to hunch to continue.

Finally the column stopped and Blondie helped the Doctor step onto its peak. She pointed at another box hanging in the air, and the pillar began to extend. It carried them slowly upwards through another glass floor until they were standing in the office of the Chief Architect.

CHAPTER 14
THE ARCHITECT

The office was large and sprawling and the walls seemed to be covered in a patchwork of red shapes that made it hard to tell just how large the room was. In the centre of the room, the Chief Architect was playing a piano. His fingers danced over the keys and the notes rang out in the silence – each one changing the shade of a shape on the wall. Then the Architect saw the Doctor and Blondie standing in front of him and raised his hands from the keyboard. Slowly, the colours faded. The deep reds washed away to white and even the piano seemed to melt into an orange skeleton before folding itself into the floor.

'Doctor,' he said quietly, a soft smile on his face. 'I've heard all about you.'

The Doctor swayed on his heels. 'I hope it was good things,' he replied, offering his hand for the Architect to shake.

'Of course,' said the Architect. He was young, with white hair that matched his shirt and grey trousers that matched his shoes. But even though he was small, his power could be felt in every aspect of his office, bubbling away beneath the surface.

'I'm sorry if this is rude,' the Doctor frowned for a moment, 'but aren't you a little young to be the Chief Architect?'

The Architect raised his eyebrows. 'Our age isn't revealed in our faces, Doctor, we have so many other ways of showing our wisdom.' He leaned forward. 'But I don't think I'm the only person in this room who is older than he looks, am I?'

The Doctor grinned. 'You're good, very good.'

The Architect shrugged. 'I know.'

Blondie stepped forward. When she spoke her words were filled with a respect that the Doctor hadn't seen from her before. 'Can you help us, sir?'

The Architect looked away. He moved his fingers ever-so-slightly and suddenly the walls of the room fell away to reveal the landscape beyond. In the far distance, the familiar darkness was approaching, a black smudge in the green sky. 'I don't know,' he said sadly. 'Even I don't have the power to hold back the destruction of our world.'

Blondie reached out her hand to grab the Doctor's. 'The Doctor has a plan.'

The Doctor shifted on his feet for a moment. 'Sort of.'

Blondie stared at him.

'What?' said the Doctor, defensively, 'I never said I could stop the system wipe – the best I can do is to buy us some time.'

'But you said –' Blondie looked shocked.

'What do you need, Doctor?' the Architect interrupted.

The Doctor leaned forward. 'I need you to make me something. I'm only a new player. I don't have the levels or the experience for, well, anything really. But you, you know the system inside out; you can find shortcuts and program new codes. Give me the power to change the objects in this world and I promise I will do everything I can to save it.'

The Architect nodded. 'You are a brave man, Doctor. We have spent so long living in peace that some of us have forgotten how to fight. Except you,' he looked at Blondie. 'It is good to see you happy again.'

'I'm not happy, I'm terrified,' said Blondie.

'With you, I think it's hard to tell the difference.'

A smile tugged at the corners of Blondie's mouth, but the Doctor clapped his hands together before she could reply. 'Right!' he declared. 'Let's get started!'

CHAPTER 15
CHEAT

The Doctor's explanation had taken nearly half an hour to complete. The air around the Chief Architect had become filled with a rainbow of plans, drawings and lists of abilities that the Doctor required. Now the Doctor and Blondie had retreated to the far corner of the office, where the Architect had conjured up a small table and two armchairs to keep them out of his way while he began to create.

The Doctor sipped a small cup of what looked like tea, but it tasted of nothing and smelled of even less.

'Why do you drink that?' Blondie asked

him. She'd brought her sword onto her lap and was polishing it vigorously.

'In the real world this would smell of something,' the Doctor replied mournfully, 'something comforting and calming.'

'Smell?'

'Obviously two senses were missed out when this virtual world was created.'

Blondie frowned. 'You mean there are more than three?'

The Doctor nodded. 'There are five, usually, sometimes more.'

Blondie laughed. 'That seems far too many to keep track of. No wonder the humans have never really explored what they could do with sight or sound. They must be in a constant state of confusion.'

'You know, I think you must be right.' The Doctor smiled and took another sip of his flavourless drink.

Blondie looked over to where the Architect

was standing in a whirlwind of computer code. His hands darted around the swirling fragments, pulling lines from the air and mixing them with others. Textures and sounds were created and then pulled into the central shape. Others were dismissed with a wave of the Architect's hand, crumbling into numbers on the floor.

Sparks were flying as the object neared completion and the office became a collage of colours – blues and greens, reds and oranges. They merged into rainbows and then a pure white light. Eventually, the Architect was finished.

The Doctor applauded loudly as he got to his feet to meet the man. Blondie blinked, surprised at how quickly the all-powerful wizard she had seen while he worked had returned to the mild young man they had first met.

'Stunning,' was all the Doctor could say when he came face to face with the Chief Architect.

The Architect bowed his head. 'We all have things we're good at, Doctor. My skills are just particularly flashy.'

'Did you manage it?' asked the Doctor.

'Yes.'

The Architect held out his hands and presented the Doctor with his request. 'It's a clever design,' he commented, 'capable of tampering with even the most complicated of codes. If these weren't desperate times, then I would have refused to grant such an outrageous request. I shudder to think what would happen if this fell into the wrong hands.'

'Don't you worry about that,' the Doctor grasped the item firmly. 'I'm very protective of my sonic screwdriver.'

'Your what?' Blondie peered over his shoulder.

'Sonic screwdriver.' The Doctor flourished the device triumphantly. He thumbed a catch and the handle snapped open to reveal a glowing green crystal. He grinned slyly. 'My all-purpose tampering device.'

'What's sonic about it?'

'Nothing,' the Architect wiped his hands with a handkerchief, then made it vanish. 'It's a cheat code actually — but its appearance was based on the Doctor's description. It allows him to tamper with the computer code that makes up our world; to change it and exaggerate it. He can make it do whatever he likes. But without something for it to tamper with, it's virtually useless.'

'That's what I like about it. It's a tool not a weapon. Tools make other things work better.'

'How appropriate for a man named Doctor,' said the Architect.

'So, what's the plan?' asked Blondie.

'First I need to test a theory,' the Doctor turned to her. 'Your navigation thing, the spell that showed us the way to the Architects' Guild. It can show you the route to anywhere in Parallife, right?'

'Right.'

'Which means that somewhere in that spell is a world map?'

'I guess so.'

The Doctor flicked on the sonic screwdriver. 'Then let's bring it up.'

Blondie knew what to do. She flexed her hands, summoning the white ball of lightning once again. But before she could cast it into the air, the Doctor's screwdriver let out a high-pitched whir.

The ball expanded and shifted, transforming into a metre wide, three-dimensional shape full of kinks and planes and smooth curves.

The Doctor leaned forward to examine it and his nose almost touched the shimmering image. 'So this is what Parallife looks like,' he murmured. 'But it didn't always look like this, did it?'

'No. We Architects have adjusted the landscape, changing it to suit the needs of the citizens in each area. The largest towers are easier to build if the world is flat, whereas others prefer a traditional, curved horizon.'

'Yeah.' The Doctor nodded, 'that sounds about right. But what happens if I hammer out the kinks?' He activated the sonic screwdriver again, and gradually the shape began to shift once more – smoothing it out until it became a perfect sphere. 'There we go,' he smiled, 'the original globe.'

Blondie shrugged. 'So it's more round, what's the big deal?'

The Doctor glanced over his shoulder. 'Nothing, to you. But what you don't know is that the human world outside of Parallife is also a sphere.' He pointed at the glowing outlines of Parallife's continents. 'And although the Architects have changed your world dramatically since the players left, the basic shapes of the digital continents are the same. Parallife is an almost exact copy of planet Earth!'

He jammed his screwdriver into the image and immediately it grew, zooming into a particular city. 'I thought I recognized the road layouts beneath the Guild – we're in Atlanta!'

'Atlanta?'

'That's the Earth-name for it; it's a city in America.'

'America?'

The Doctor sighed. He was getting nowhere fast. 'Okay, back to basics,' he said, straightening up. 'Parallife is a copy of Earth, right?' the pair nodded. 'And the system wipe is being caused by something in the real world – right? A computer or an artificial intelligence or something,' they nodded again. 'So, if we can find the centre of the system wipe in Parallife, then that will tell us the Earth-location of the computer that's causing it. We can turn it off!'

'But even if we found out where that was, how would we reach it, Doctor?' said the Architect, 'None of us exist in the outside world.'

'Leave that to me,' said the Doctor. He turned to Blondie. 'So, this spell of yours, it creates a path to whatever location you choose?'

'I just need to say the word,' she replied.

'And if that location's been wiped then it won't be able to give you directions to it, yes?'

'I guess not, I've not tried.'

The Doctor smiled. 'Well, ask it now. Ask it to give you directions to everywhere!'

Blondie raised an eyebrow, but she was already too confused to risk asking another question. She leant forward into the spell and spoke a single word. Suddenly the image was covered in bright white streaks. They layered themselves over the continents, lighting up the Architect's office until the entire globe was covered. But there was a section missing – a dull orange area of the map that the white streaks refused to enter. A hole in the world.

'There it is,' the Doctor looked grim. 'Anything that the spell can't show us a path to has been erased. Now I just need to find the centre of the hole.' He twisted the screwdriver one final time and the globe expanded once more. It grew to fill the room until the Doctor, Blondie and the Chief Architect were standing in the exact centre of the hole in the map. The Doctor examined it.

'Oklahoma?' he frowned. 'Really?'

CHAPTER 16
A MESSAGE

'Is this a button?'

'I dunno, press it.'

'You press it.' Rory took a step back from Daryl's screen, worried that he might touch something dangerous.

Amy pushed him aside and put an ear to his chest. The speaker was still ringing loudly in the gloom. 'There's got to be something we can do to answer the call.'

'Maybe it's not a call, maybe Daryl thinks that's music.'

Amy sighed. 'Somehow I don't think that's true.'

Rory tugged her shoulder and pulled her

back to stand beside him. 'Here, let me try something,' he said.

Amy looked at him expectantly.

Rory cleared his throat. 'Uh, hello?'

Daryl's screen flashed into life.

'Wow, I didn't think that would work.' Rory grinned. But his smile soon vanished as a series of large red letters began to scroll across the screen.

USER ERROR REPORT INCOMING, it said, ACCEPT OR REJECT?

'Um, accept, I guess.' Rory swallowed.

The screen went blank for a moment, then a familiar face faded into view.

'Doctor!' Amy shouted. 'You're alive!'

'Well of course I'm alive,' said the Doctor, his voice crackling through Daryl's speaker. 'Why wouldn't I be?'

'You . . .' Amy trailed off. 'You almost died Doctor!'

'Where?'

'In the apartment block! There was an army of demolition robots – they're tearing up the world!'

On the screen the Doctor checked himself, patting his shirt down quickly. 'Well, I can't be dead in the real world or else I'd be dead in here now, wouldn't I?'

'Yeah, congratulations on the virtual body by the way,' Rory interrupted, 'much less . . . chinny.'

'Oi!' said the Doctor.

'Okay,' Amy held up a calming hand. 'We've not got time for this.'

'No, exactly,' replied the Doctor, rubbing his chin. 'So if the apartment block's been destroyed, where are you now?'

'We were rescued.'

'Rescued? By whom?'

'Daryl, he's a robot, that's how you're speaking to us – through his face. I'm not going to lie Doctor,' Amy looked at Daryl's hunched body, still posed in sleep-mode, 'it's kinda weird.' She shivered.

On the screen the Doctor thought for a moment. 'Interesting,' he muttered. 'Did he tell you where he was from?'

'No, we don't know much about him apart from that he saved our lives.'

'And that he doesn't know what humans look like,' Rory interrupted. 'He seems to be on the run from this Legacy thing as well.'

On the screen the Doctor thought for a moment. 'Also interesting,' he muttered.

'So how did you find us?' Rory continued.

'I didn't,' said the Doctor. 'I found a way to cheat the system.' He held up his sonic screwdriver. 'I sent an error report to the outside world. It's programmed to appear on any screen still connected to the network – I thought you'd still be looking over my shoulder in Chicago.'

'Why's Daryl connected to the network?'

Amy flashed Rory a look. Rory shrugged.

'Beats me.'

The Doctor shook his head in disbelief. 'Things are getting stranger by the minute.' He looked up again. 'Right, we need to focus.'

'What do you need us to do?' Amy was ready immediately.

'There's a system wipe erasing Parallife.'

'Parallife?'

'This place, the virtual world. It's modelled on Earth, except that now all the humans have gone, the players' characters have been doing a bit of . . . redecoration.'

'Gotcha,' Amy said.

'But something's trying to delete the whole thing, trying to reboot the system. I don't know why. But you need to get to the central computer and stop it.'

Rory cleared his throat. Amy and the Doctor looked at him. 'Would this central computer be called Legacy by any chance?'

'Maybe, I don't know.'

'Because the same kind of thing is happening out here, Doctor. Daryl called it a restoration. They're going to demolish the planet and then rebuild it.'

The Doctor slapped his head. 'Of course! That's what it is! The system wipe must be mapped onto the path of the demolition. Legacy is destroying both the virtual world and the real world at the same time. It's a reset program, ready to make Earth inhabitable for humanity when they return – Internet and everything.'

'But Daryl doesn't know whether the humans are ever going to return.'

'You can't take the word of one robot,' the Doctor replied. 'They could be taking shelter out in space for all we know.'

'Doctor, outside!' a second voice crackled over Daryl's speaker, and Amy raised her eyebrows as a beautiful young woman strode into the camera's view.

'I'm coming,' the Doctor replied.

'I leave you alone for one minute,' Amy grinned, 'and look, you've gone and found a replacement.'

The Doctor rolled his eyes and chose to ignore her. 'Okay, Amy, Rory, this is the plan. I've hacked the system to find Legacy's location. You need to get there and switch it off before it completes the wipe.'

A map replaced the Doctor's face briefly, tracing a path to Oklahoma across the American desert. Amy looked for Chicago on the map and her face fell.

'But that's back the way we came. You want us to get past the demolition army?!'

'At least when the robots have passed there's still ground to walk on,' the Doctor replied. 'Here there's nothing. Literally nothing.'

'We'll try our best, Doctor,' said Rory. Amy looked at him with quiet admiration.

'And you,' she turned back to the screen, 'you need to get out of there. Find a save-point and get out of Parallife as quickly as possible.'

The Doctor looked away. 'No,' he said.

'No?!'

'I'm not leaving these people to die.'

'But they're not alive, Doctor,' Amy shouted, 'they're characters in a computer game! You're the only person in there who's real!'

The Doctor's eyes narrowed. 'They think for themselves, they imagine, they have lives like yours. Just because they exist inside an artificial world doesn't mean they're not real.'

'But in a few hours that world won't exist anymore, and you'll be trapped inside it with no way of escape,' said Amy.

'Not if you get to Legacy in time. Until then I have to do everything I can to save them.'

'But what's the use of saving people if there's nowhere left for them to live?' Amy didn't understand.

The Doctor squeezed his forehead in confusion at a half-remembered thought. 'I'm working on it,' he said finally.

'Doctor!' the woman's voice shouted again.

'I said I'm coming!' the Doctor called over his shoulder. He turned back to the screen. 'I'm going to leave an error message on the network – when you get to Legacy use it to find me.'

He raised his hand to the screen and the image vanished.

'Oh, great.' Rory stomped over to the double doors of the bunker, staring out into the evening sunlight.

'We've got to find a way through the army,' Amy replied.

'Yeah, well that's fun to say, but how?'

'I think I might be able to help.' The pair spun around to find Daryl jerking his body into motion with a grinding hiss of gears.

'Did you . . . ?' Rory trailed off.

'Did you hear what the Doctor was saying?' Amy finished for him.

Daryl nodded, his screen displaying the now-familiar smiling face.

'Those things we said about you,' Rory began, 'we didn't mean anything bad by them, you know.'

Daryl shrugged noisily. 'In a time like this, there is no need for manners.' He swung his screen slowly between the pair. 'Although they cost nothing.'

Rory shuffled and looked at his feet.

'Did you know about the system wipe, Daryl?' Amy asked.

'No,' he replied. 'It is a shame.'

'Why?'

'Parallife was a wonderful place. I'll be sad to see it go.'

'You've been there?'

'I was Parallife.'

'What?'

'But I'm not any more.' Daryl dismissed the question and walked over to the doors. He looked out and his yellow face fell. 'My jump is powerful, and my speed is second to none, but I'm afraid that the chances of our survival are small if we attempt to break through with you two on my back. The strength of the storm would kill you, let alone the robots themselves.'

'Tell me about it,' Rory said.

'We need to think.' Amy buried her head in her hands. 'It's not just our lives at stake, it's the Doctor's and everyone else in that world.'

'We could stay here and wait for the army to pass over the bunker before we head out. It'd be plain sailing after that,' Rory said.

'That could be hours,' Amy replied. 'Who knows how many people would die in Parallife before we left? We need to leave now . . .' Her sentence faded away to silence. Daryl and Rory looked at her expectantly. 'Wait,' she raised her head. 'I've got it.'

CHAPTER 17
A PLAN

They climbed the metal walkways to the roof of the bunker once again, and Daryl plunged his hand into one of the computer controls that lined the highest walkway. The building shuddered and creaked, ancient winches grinding into motion.

In front of them, the huge metal bulk of a sleeping robot began to tremble and sway. Then the chains that fastened it to the ceiling began to give, winding across the gears until they caught. Slowly, the sleeping monster began to descend.

Daryl withdrew his hand and nodded to Amy and Rory. No one bothered to speak over the noise.

Soon the highest point of the construction robot had lowered past the top-most walkway and the pair began to walk quickly down the steps to keep level with it. Turning across the walkways and down the flights of stairs, they kept their eyes fastened on the metal bulk beside them.

Four floors down, the noise of the machinery had quietened enough for them to talk.

'So how does this help?' Rory asked.

Amy folded her arms in frustration. 'Isn't it obvious?'

'Well no, or I wouldn't have asked.'

'We're safe inside this bunker because the demolition army are programmed to avoid the construction robots, right? As well as everything a construction robot builds.'

'Okay.'

'So if we want to get through the army's front line, we need something that they won't just trample straight over.'

Rory's face lit up. 'Like a construction robot!'

'Exactly. With Daryl's help we can get our over-sized friend here to build a road all the way to Legacy!'

Rory looked behind them, back up the way they had come. 'Yeah . . . where is Daryl anyway?'

By now the construction robot's front limbs and tracks had reached the floor and the creature's tail end was gradually being laid down behind it. There was a heavy thud as the rear caterpillar tracks hit the floor, supporting the last few tonnes of the robot's incredible weight.

Suddenly, a flash of white metal flew past the walkway where Amy and Rory had paused. It smacked into the rear of the monster and unfurled slowly – Daryl. He got to his feet and began to unfasten the chains from the construction robot's body.

'Oh, I see,' said Rory, 'He took the short cut.'

When they reached the cool metal of the bunker's floor, the construction robot had already been freed. Daryl sat astride its tree trunk neck, waiting for them.

He pointed to the rungs of a small maintenance ladder that snaked up the side of the robot's body, and together they hauled themselves onto its back.

They found themselves on top of a large, flat surface covered in hatches. Each one was the size of a small car, and each had been spray-painted with a now-peeling white number. Rusting track marks traced away from them to meet the main piston arms of the construction robot. The arms arced away into the darkness like the wings of a giant metal dragon, folded over the rows of tracks and legs that were designed to carry the robot's weight.

'Hold onto something,' Daryl called from

his perch further along.

Rory didn't need telling twice. He lodged himself between two steel bolts, each as big as himself, in the shadow of a metal shoulder blade. He was careful not to stand within reach of the mechanical arms. Amy joined him, picking her way awkwardly over the hatches.

'Ready?' Daryl shouted.

Rory raised his thumb over the ledge.

The construction robot shuddered into motion with such force that Amy and Rory were nearly thrown from their perch. They scrambled for grip on the rusted metal surface, their hands turning red as the rust flaked away. Behind them, two of the hatches began to roll open – revealing two churning vats of tarmac. As they watched, the boiling liquid began to overflow, running into shallow troughs that ran the length of the robot's back. The liquid bubbled and gurgled, slowly flowing into a series of large holes and down into the inner workings of the construction robot.

The smell of cooling tar invaded Rory's nostrils and he screwed up his nose at the stench. Amy pulled on his arm, pointing over the side of the robot and over towards the doors of the bunker. He followed her gaze. A large, ink-black pool was spreading across the floor, sprayed from nozzles in the robot's chest. As they watched, the great metal arms swung up and over on their creaking joints. They carved the pool of tarmac into a sharp rectangle as wide as the robot itself.

Then, with another violent jolt, the robot jerked into motion. Its tracks began to move and slowly it inched forwards onto the tarmac. A sticky, tearing noise echoed throughout the bunker as the construction robot began to flatten the liquid road in front of it, as it rolled towards the bunker's doors.

Daryl gripped the rear of the robot's head with both hands. He plugged his fingers into the circuits of its artificial brain, guiding the monster and overriding the preprogrammed instructions. He set a course for Oklahoma.

With an almighty crash, the construction robot collided with the bunker doors, bending the metal outwards as if it were cardboard. Sparks streamed across the bodywork as it squeezed out into the open air. A hail of golden light showered Amy and Rory as they passed through.

Then they were free.

The pair whooped for joy, hugging each other as the construction robot mounted the first dune. Behind them the black trail of a road stretched through the dark opening of the bunker, and in front of them the lay the desert.

'Are we going to make it?' Rory said, squeezing Amy's hand tightly.

She turned her face to the horizon, and the angry boil of the sandstorm in the distance. It was miles away now, but growing closer with every passing second.

'We have to,' she replied.

CHAPTER 18
BATTLEGROUND

The frozen image of Amy and Rory's anxious faces still hung in the air in the Architect's office. The Doctor looked at it sadly, then grasped a corner with his thumb. He shrank the picture down until it was the size of a small photograph, then folded it neatly and stuck it in his pocket.

'What is it?' he turned to where Blondie and the Chief Architect were standing. Behind them the wall of the office had been removed to reveal the eerily quiet landscape of Parallife.

'There,' Blondie pointed.

The Doctor looked.

'Oh, oh dear.'

'I know.'

Beyond the city borders, an army was approaching. An orange trail of numbers fell away behind them as they marched towards the Guild. The Doctor winced at the sight of the screaming broken shapes that writhed on the front line and looked away.

'What are they?' asked the Architect.

'The Defrags,' Blondie replied. 'The heralds of the darkness.'

'They're what remains of your work.' The Doctor's eyes narrowed. 'All of your wonderful creations, all your improvements, broken by the system wipe. They are all that's left of the Games Master's gift of intelligence after the original programming has been destroyed.'

'You mean, they're people?' the Architect gasped.

'Trapped inside the fragments of your new graphics,' the Doctor nodded.

Blondie turned to him, raising her hand to

the sword hilt on her back. 'We have to,' she said.

'I know,' replied the Doctor.

'Have to what?' the Architect looked from one to the other.

'We have to fight,' Blondie said. 'If we don't they'll destroy the city before the darkness even reaches us.'

The Architect looked at the Doctor. 'But if what you say is true, Doctor, then they don't know what they're doing! They're innocent!'

'I know,' the Doctor said again. 'But we've run out of options. We have to buy Amy and Rory some time.'

'But you said you'd save us, Doctor, whatever it takes.'

The Doctor looked grim. 'I know, but –'

He paused.

Then his face lit up. 'Of course, it's obvious!'

'What is?' Blondie asked.

But the Doctor was already heading towards the central lift. 'You'll find out,' he winked. 'Blondie, come with me. We've got a war to win.'

'Now you're talking.' Blondie strode over to stand behind him, snatching her sword into her hand. She looked over to the Chief Architect. 'Coming?' she asked.

The Architect lowered his head. 'No,' he said slowly. 'All I've ever wanted, my entire life, is to create. The thought of this darkness, this destruction, is heartbreaking. I cannot bear to watch, let alone be a part of it.'

Behind him, the open wall began to reform. White blocks formed in the air outside, sliding into place until the office was enclosed once more.

The Doctor nodded. 'Thank you,' he said, 'for all your help.'

But the Architect ignored him. He took a seat on his white stool once again and held out his hands. Orange keys began to outline themselves around his outstretched fingers and the white wood of a piano started to fill in the gaps.

The lift began to move, and the Doctor and Blondie were lowered into the soft green glow of the corridor once again. Above them, the soft notes of the Architect's playing faded away into silence.

CHAPTER 19
THE SWORD AND THE SCREWDRIVER

They had only been walking down the central pillar of the Guild for ten minutes when the Doctor became frustrated. 'We don't have time for this!' he shouted, brandishing his sonic screwdriver.

He switched off the pillar's gravity.

For a split second, Blondie and the Doctor hung in space, their bodies uncertain as to which way was up. Then they were sent tumbling down towards the base of the structure.

Doors, floors and then the main hall flashed past them at incredible speed, and Blondie screamed with excitement as they continued into the depths of the Guild. The corridors narrowed once more as the opposite side of the Guild narrowed in a perfect reflection of itself and soon they were rushing towards the final floor – and the doorway to the ground.

The Doctor fumbled for his sonic screwdriver, but it slipped from his hand. It hung in the air beside him, falling at the exact same speed as he was, until the Doctor snatched it back and thumbed a button.

Almost immediately the pillar's gravity returned and the pair were dragged onto its surface. They slipped and slid across the last few metres, scrambling for a handhold. Finally they skidded to rest at the very end of the pillar.

They climbed to their feet and looked up at the floor that seemed to hang above their heads. But they were actually standing on the ceiling.

'Here, jump,' Blondie grabbed his hand and yanked him into the air. They flipped over, landing with a thud on the floor.

'Well, that was . . . confusing,' said the Doctor.

They lay there for a minute; looking up at the pillar above them, back the way they had come. It stretched away for what seemed like miles until its shape was lost in the glow.

The Doctor turned his head to look at Blondie. She turned to look at him.

'Hand me your sword,' he said.

'Why?'

'Because I'm going to save the Defrags.'

'I don't understand.' Blondie frowned, but she passed him her sword anyway.

He ran his screwdriver across the shimmering blade. The white metal rippled as the green light passed over it.

'This sword, in computer programming terms, is designed to erase the body and mind of whatever animal you strike. But every time you hit something with it, you earn experience.'

'Only from animals, not other citizens.'

'Yeah. So it's already in the sword's code to transmit something from the creature into the blade of the sword. But what if it wasn't experience points that were transmitted, what if it was people's minds? What if, with every stroke of your sword you could separate the mind of a citizen from their body and store it in the blade?'

Blondie realised what he was saying. 'You mean I could remove the minds of the Defrags. I could destroy their broken bodies but keep their minds safe?'

'Exactly. You wouldn't be killing anyone, but you'd stop them from killing others,' the Doctor said.

'You'd be literally saving them, storing them on the network. And without their bodies the system wipe wouldn't be able to touch them. Because their minds can't be erased. Doctor that's brilliant.'

The Doctor grinned. 'Well, duh.'

'But what's the point?' Blondie looked away. 'Our world will be gone, there'll be nowhere for them to live, no bodies for them to control. They'll just be stuck, in a world of nothing.'

The Doctor propped himself up on his elbows and handed the weapon back to Blondie. 'We'll see,' he said.

Blondie rolled onto her knees and looked down at the Doctor, still leaning on the floor. He was smiling quietly to himself. 'You're not telling me everything, are you Doctor?' she said.

The Doctor stopped smiling. 'I don't want to get your hopes up, Blondie,' he replied. 'But I think it all rests on Daryl.'

'Daryl? Who's Daryl?' Blondie raised her eyebrows.

'I don't know,' the Doctor jumped to his feet and strode over to a small wooden door. 'But I have a feeling . . .' He grasped the bronze doorknob firmly and pressed his ear against the wood. He listened for a moment and then shook his head.

Blondie looked at him.

The Doctor looked back at her, shrugged, and then flung open the door.

Outside, the city was in chaos. The deep green shadow of the Guild rippled across the curving buildings, as if the entire world were underwater. The air was filled with the broken gleam of numbers. They formed orange ash that drifted through the streets as the Defrags dismantled the world.

The citizens were running scared, and the Doctor and Blondie watched the confusion in silence for moment. They traced the movement of the crowds; trying to discover which direction they were running in.

Finally, Blondie pointed. 'They're running that way.'

'So the Defrags must be –'

'That way,' Blondie pointed in the opposite

direction. 'I need to get to the front line, I'm the only person who can fight these things.'

The Doctor nodded. 'Then you'd best get going.'

Blondie nodded and drew her sword, spiralling it around her body with practised ease. She tested its weight in her grip, then began to jog towards the noise of the battle.

But a few steps later, she stopped and turned.

'Wait,' she said, 'what about you?'

The Doctor put his hands in his pockets. 'What do you mean?'

'You're a player. Your mind isn't part of the network. When the time comes my sword won't save you, you'll be disconnected from your other body and die.'

'I know,' said the Doctor. 'Let's just hope it doesn't come to that.'

'If you could get to a save-point before it's too late . . .'

'I'm not leaving Parallife,' the Doctor

looked stern.

Blondie smiled. 'I know,' she said. 'But it was worth a try.'

She turned and began to run – her sword held out by her side. It flashed in the gloom for a moment and then was lost in the crowd.

When the Doctor was sure she was out of sight he reached into his pocket. He pulled out the picture of Amy and Rory and unfolded it carefully. 'Come on, you two,' he muttered, 'save my life.'

CHAPTER 20
BREAKTHROUGH

The sandstorm loomed large in the sky above Amy and Rory, and even the bulk of the construction robot was dwarfed by its size. They were barely a mile away from the front line but already the sand around the construction robot's tracks was churning. The wind was intense and Amy and Rory covered their mouths, hiding their faces in their shoulders to escape the stinging grains.

Even the steady flow of tarmac was warping and twisting as it failed to find steady ground on the dune – despite the best efforts of the construction robot's mechanical arms.

Daryl gave up his seat on the robot's neck

and walked along its back to meet the pair. They looked up at the sound of his footsteps.

'This is going to get bumpy,' he shouted over the noise of the wind.

'Yeah, we kinda got that,' Rory mouthed over to him.

Daryl stepped around them and held out his arms as wide as he could, fastening his hands onto the metal on either side of them with a burst of white heat. With a series of soft pops his exoskeleton opened slightly, fanning out to create a protective barrier around the pair.

He began to speak but the noise was too loud, so instead his words were displayed in text across his screen.

'Hold on tight.'

A deep bass rumble was beginning now, the sound of the demolition robots hidden behind their tidal wave of destruction. It was a terrifying, clanking growl, as if the angry pistons were fighting each other for the chance to disintegrate the construction robot and its crew.

Then the storm hit them.

The construction robot rocked like a boat in the crashing waves of sand that engulfed it. Pale white showers of dust washed over its bodywork and choked its fragile passengers.

Amy tried to open her eyes but couldn't. The sand clung too tightly to her face and she dared not breathe for fear of drowning in the grit.

A noise like a buzz saw erupted all around them as the tarmac pumps became clogged and overflowed. Amy and Rory managed to grab onto Daryl's arms and pull themselves up just in time to avoid a searing flood of hot tar. It flowed across the construction robot's back and onto the struggling tracks beneath it.

Then the robot lurched one more time and levelled out.

The storm was calmer here and Amy risked

letting go of Daryl's shoulder to wipe her face and look back the way they had come.

'We've passed the demolition zone.' The text scrolled across Daryl's screen, but it wasn't needed. Amy could see that for herself. Behind them, the rambling tarmac path that had trailed behind them for so long had suddenly straightened out, as the ground around it smoothed. Gone were the rough hills of the dunes, instead replaced with a smooth, flat, gritted wasteland.

Amy moved her head slowly upwards. The swirling sands blotted out the sun, and the world was tinged in browns and golds. Then she saw them, the demolition robots, huge outlines in the darkness.

If she hadn't known what they were she would have guessed that they were giants. Dark, lumbering shapes the size of skyscrapers moved slowly behind a curtain of sand. Even the sound of their destruction was faded here, and it seemed to Amy as if the demolition robots walked in silence. Like ghosts in the storm.

She breathed.

And the sand came crashing down once more.

CHAPTER 21
LEGACY

'Amy? Amy!' Rory slapped her gently round the face to wake her up.

'What? What is it?' Amy mumbled. She tried to get up from where she was lying, but found that her clothes had stuck to the drying tarmac that lined the rear of the robot. She yanked, hard, and winced as she heard her jacket rip. Then she realised that it was night. 'How long was I asleep?' she asked, suddenly awake.

Rory grinned. 'Almost the entire trip, you lucky thing. It was well boring,' he turned and pointed at the perfectly straight road stretching away behind them.

'So we're here?' she asked, looking around.

'Oklahoma?'

'Where the wind comes sweepin' down the plain.'

'It's a bit . . . flat.'

'Everything is flat now,' said Daryl, looking down from his perch on top of the ledge. 'This is fertile ground, ready to be rebuilt. And that —' He turned his head and pointed in front of them, 'is Legacy.'

Amy and Rory both scrambled onto the ledge as the construction robot trundled onwards. When Amy finally hauled herself onto the cool, unstained metal at its front, the sight before her made her catch her breath.

'It's huge,' she said quietly.

'Well, it needed to house an army,' Rory replied.

A gigantic, stepped pyramid rose into the sky in front of them, and its black polished surface reflected the stars. As the robot approached, they could see the chambers that must once have housed the demolition robots – dark, shadowy holes that lined the lower hundred storeys. At the top of the pyramid a ribbed transmission mast cast a moon-like spotlight across the desert. A lighthouse in the wilderness.

'Do you think the future has anything that's normal-sized?' said Rory eventually.

Amy shook her head.

They sat together, watching the pyramid grow as they approached it. Daryl busied himself with the robot's controls, turning it slightly towards one of the glass lifts that sat patiently at the bottom of the structure.

Eventually the construction robot reached its destination. It collided against the polished surface of Legacy with a loud crack, then shuddered to a halt.

Rory hopped down the ladder, eager to stretch his legs on solid ground. He stared at the long white scratch the robot had carved into the wall. 'I hope no one tries to send us a bill for that.'

'I'm pretty sure there's no one round here to tell on us.' Amy jogged over to the lift. She pulled open the double glass doors and peered inside. 'Uh, Daryl – I'm not sure you're going to fit.'

'Don't worry about me,' Daryl replied. 'I'll ride on top.' He reached up to the roof of the lift and pulled himself onto its thin metal ceiling. It bent slightly, but held his weight.

Amy nodded. 'Are you okay?' she asked. 'You've been . . . quiet. For a while now.'

Daryl nodded and looked away.

Amy decided not to press him any further and motioned for Rory to join her in the lift.

'I hate glass lifts,' he muttered, stepping inside and closing the door. 'Why does anyone think you want to see how far away the ground is?'

Amy sighed and pressed a button. The doors hissed shut and the lift began to climb.

Rory buried his face in his shirt and refused to look until they reached the top.

As they reached the final floor, another pair of glass doors opened onto the central control chamber. At this height the pyramid had narrowed, but the chamber was still the size of a small shopping centre.

The polished black surface continued inside, coating the floors and the low ceiling. The room was lit by moonlight. It flooded through the windows that lined every wall. But the room was so large that it was unable to illuminate the very centre of the structure.

Amy's stubby heels clicked loudly on the floor as she entered, followed by Rory. She walked over to the shadowy central area. As she did so, the floor and ceiling began to glow softly. They cast a calming natural light and the shadows fell away as she approached. They revealed a curving Desktop computer, above which hung a variety of different-sized monitors. The central hub.

She reached out her hand and ran it over the ebony surface of the Desktop. It blossomed into life. Ripples of colour spread out across the surface, spilling onto the floor around her.

'The whole room is a Desktop!' Amy cried.

'I know,' said Rory. 'You've had a message floating by your feet the entire time.' He looked around to where Daryl had sent the lift sliding slowly back down the outside of the building so that he could enter through the glass doors. 'Come on Daryl, we haven't got all day!'

Amy had to crouch to read the words that floated in the floor by her feet in small red letters. ERROR REPORT FILED. They said.

'This must be the Doctor's message,' she edged closer towards the curving Desktop, and managed to get close enough that the letters flowed up and onto the surface. She pointed a finger and jabbed at the words.

The screens above her head lit up, each one opening the message simultaneously. But instead of the Doctor's comforting face, all that appeared was a string of yellow text.

Is Daryl the Games Master?

Love

the Doctor

'What does it mean?' said Rory, squinting.

Amy turned to where the large bulk of Daryl's figure was hidden in the shadows near the door. 'Well?' she asked him.

Daryl's screen switched on and a sad yellow face appeared.

'Yes,' he said.

CHAPTER 22
MISTAKEN IDENTITY

'I was the first,' Daryl began. He leaned heavily against the central Desktop, as if suddenly tired. Amy wondered how long it would be able to take his weight. 'The first artificial intelligence in Parallife. The game had been going so long that all the players had seen nearly everything the level designers had created. So they created me to build new levels and new monsters – new adventures for the players to have. My job was to see everything, check on everyone – to make sure each of their character's stories were exciting and thrilling. Then one day, they just left.'

He raised his head to the ceiling. As if it

were aware of his motion, the display above him blossomed into an image of the sky. A bright sun, clouds and behind them an impossibly blue sky lit up the control room.

'I didn't know where. I didn't know how. But they vanished and Parallife was left empty. All those adventures I'd created and the characters that had experienced them. They'd all just stopped, their stories left unfinished. I couldn't bear it.'

Above him the sky shifted and changed, the day turning to night and then back to day again, over and over – time passing at high speed.

'It was ten years before I came upon a solution,' Daryl continued. 'I took my mind and copied it. Then placed the copies inside the players' characters and each version of me changed to suit their body. My mind was limitless; I wasn't trapped inside a body. But with my mind in a million different characters – it adapted to fit each one. They developed into personalities. Then they began to create. They made their own levels, crafted new monsters, found new ways to communicate. For the first time since the game began their stories were truly their own. It was then that I realised I wasn't needed any more.'

'So you left them?' Rory interrupted. 'On their own?'

Daryl nodded. 'I'm a tinkerer, my job was to interfere. But now I couldn't interfere – it wouldn't be fair. I wanted to let them make their own mistakes, and create their own rewards. So I left Parallife and found a way to download my mind into the body of a robot. Now I'm like them, trapped inside a body, in a world I don't know anything about.' The smiley face appeared. 'It's wonderful.'

'So that's why you'd never seen a human before – your only experience of them was in the game. You didn't know what they might look like in the real world.'

'Exactly,' said Daryl. 'When I left, the only things on the planet were robots. I thought they might be humans. For a while I thought I might be human.'

On the ceiling, the sun set one final time and the sky faded away to nothing. Daryl got to his feet.

'You have to go back to Parallife,' Amy said. 'You have to save them. Stop the system wipe! You're the only one of us who knows how.'

'No.' Daryl held up his large metal hands and backed away, 'I can't.'

'Why not?'

'Because of what I said. Once I'm inside the system I'm too powerful. If I start acting like a god then the characters will stop being free to create their own destinies – I'll be like a human, directing my creations as I see fit. If they don't have the imagination to save themselves, then I have failed.'

He looked away and strode loudly over to

the window.

Amy looked at Rory. He shrugged.

'I will save the Doctor,' Daryl said eventually, 'Because he is not my creation. I can create a save-point for him to escape through.'

'But if you do that the Doctor's efforts will be wasted. He's risking his life to save your characters!'

Daryl said nothing.

'Daryl, if you don't do it, I'll have to do it myself,' Amy shouted. 'And I don't know what any of this stuff does. Who knows what I'll blow up!'

Rory put his hand on Amy's shoulder. 'Let me try,' he whispered. She looked at him in confusion, but hung back.

Slowly, Rory walked over to the window and stood beside Daryl. Neither of them looked at each other.

'You're thinking about this all wrong, Daryl,' Rory said, gazing out over the landscape. 'You think too much of yourself.'

Still Daryl didn't reply.

'Just because you created them doesn't make you their god,' he paused. 'It makes you their father.' He turned to look at the large screen of Daryl's face. It was blank, and gave no clue as to what he was thinking. 'They're your children, Daryl. Save them, stop the wipe. Help them grow!'

CHAPTER 23
THE VIRTUAL WAR

The world was ending, and Blondie was having the time of her life.

She darted gracefully onto the top of a nearby building as a second wave of Defrags crashed through the city suburbs and over the remains of their fallen comrades. That had been Blondie's doing.

She paused for a moment, taking in every detail of her surroundings. The neon-framed buildings around her lay empty. The violence of the Defrag's attack and her relentless response had been enough to persuade any citizens that they had no choice but to run for their lives.

Blondie took a deep breath and plunged into the fray once more.

Her blade flashed and sliced through the ranks. All around her the twisted bodies splintered, spraying her with orange data. They tried to dodge, their broken faces howling in frustration, but she was fast. Faster than any of them.

The ranks fell and she sprinted on across the infected suburbs, smashing through the black-stained walls and corrupted gardens that stood in her way, in a white flurry of destruction.

A familiar static hiss sounded loud above her and she raised her sword. Without even looking, she spun the blade like a helicopter rotor, as a horde of Defrags plunged out of the sky towards her. They shattered on impact in a blistering Catherine wheel of pixels. Her blade glowed as more minds were absorbed.

Before the Defrag's bodies had even fallen

to the floor, she leapt high into the air once more, scattering fragments in all directions. Her eyes flashed, searching for another group to save.

Then the buildings went dark.

A shadow was cast across the city, deeper and darker than any that the Guild above could create. The angry smile on Blondie's face vanished, and she looked out across the number-soaked battlefield to the wall of darkness that dwarfed the world.

A tidal wave of pixels was gathering at its base. Made from the torn-up remains of the outlying towns. The broken pieces mixed together, churning into a multicoloured flood. The wave collected itself as the darkness advanced ever closer, gathering itself up until it arced over Blondie's head.

Then the wave broke and she was snatched from the sky.

The Doctor was running out of time.

He'd lost Blondie in the chaos of battle. Now he needed her more than ever. Looking round he spotted a spiralling staircase wrapped tightly around a sixty-metre tall golden statue of a muscle-bound man wearing a shirt and trousers. It took a moment for the Doctor to realise that it was supposed to be the Chief Architect.

He sprinted up the steps as fast as he could. At the top, he grasped the statue's outstretched arm for balance as he paused to catch his breath.

The system wipe had arrived.

It crashed into the outskirts of the city, flooding the suburbs with pixels. The Doctor looked away, and then up.

Above him the Architects' Guild was swaying on its pillar in the storm of fragmented computer code that raced across the sky. As he watched, the edge of the darkness hit its central rim, tearing up the base-codes that supported the structure. The glass flooring splintered and shattered, transforming into a hail of numbers as it fell towards the Doctor. The Guild lurched – swaying in the hurricane. Then finally the connecting pillar snapped.

'Blondie!' the Doctor shouted, desperately looking around. 'Where are you?'

The Guild toppled, away from the void. To the Doctor it seemed to fall in slow motion, the far edge of the building crashing into the centre of the city over a mile away. Almost a minute before the rest of the spires hit. The explosions rippled towards him, throwing up blinding clouds of debris.

'Blondie!' the Doctor yelled once more, hoping that she wasn't trapped beneath the wireframe rubble.

Finally, his call was answered.

'I'm here!' the Doctor turned to see the warrior standing astride one of the tower blocks above him. Her clothes were torn and stained with orange numbers, but her sword glowed brighter than ever, and her face wore a grin of triumph.

The Doctor waved, beckoning for her to join him.

She flexed her knees and jumped. Soaring through the air like a dancer, before landing by his side.

'How many?' the Doctor asked.

'At least a thousand,' she replied, looking at her sword.

'A thousand?' the Doctor looked incredulous. 'How did you manage that?'

Blondie grinned at him. 'I'm the best.'

The Doctor smiled slightly. 'I forget you can fly.'

'I can do a lot of things without you slowing me down.' Blondie winked.

A spray of pixels slashed across their faces and the Doctor ducked to avoid one of the

Defrags as it flew past them.

Blondie's sword flashed in the air for a second and the Defrag's splintered body dissolved, crumbling to join the pixels on the street below.

'Make that one thousand and one saved,' she declared, as her sword absorbed the glowing white ball that contained the citizen's mind.

The wall of darkness was closer than ever now and it filled the sky, turning the world to night. The Doctor placed a hand on Blondie's arm before she could take off again. 'No, it's too late, that'll have to do.'

Blondie stopped. 'What now? We can't outrun it.'

'I know,' he looked at her. 'Cast your water shield.'

Blondie nodded, and raised her hand.

The bright column of light arced out above them, then exploded outwards into a fountain of water – stretching out and down to the square below.

The Doctor pulled out his sonic screwdriver and, without warning, thrust it into the column of light.

'What are you doing?' Blondie shouted over the roar of the water.

'Trying to change the computer code of the spell. If I can tweak it enough, the system wipe might not be able to erase it.'

'Well I hope you can tweak fast,' Blondie replied. 'It's going to hit us!'

The Doctor turned in time to see the Darkness engulf the square.

There was an ear-splitting crunch and the Doctor screwed up his face in pain as the world around them crumbled into nothing. The water shield boiled. Clouds of steam drifted across what was left of the square, stinging the Doctor's face as the system wipe searched for a weakness in the code.

The Doctor turned to Blondie. 'I wasn't

fast enough,' he said sadly.

'It's okay,' said Blondie, 'we all have to die sometime.'

The shield trembled and stuttered. Then the water froze in mid-air, like a shining glass bubble.

The bubble popped.

CHAPTER 24
SALVATION

'**W**e're alive,' said the Doctor.

'Don't sound too surprised,' said Blondie.

They looked around as a deathly silence fell. The square had been carved into a circle, traced by the outline of the water shield. The emerald floor radiated out only a few metres from the base of the golden statue, deep green cobbles marked out on the surface. They warped and twisted as they reached the edge of the world, falling away like a waterfall frozen in time.

The Doctor looked behind them. As if through a grey haze, what remained of Parallife still stretched away in the distance, the straight border that marked the edge of the wipe overlapped only slightly with Blondie's island. Barely enough for two people to walk across side by side. The system wipe had halted.

The Doctor burst into motion, racing down the steps to the base of the statue and across to the edge of the circle. He was moving so fast that he could barely stop himself from falling when he reached the edge.

He knelt down and put his hand out in front of him.

'They did it,' he said. 'They stopped the wipe.'

Blondie appeared by his side. 'And only just in time.'

She looked down at the emptiness that stretched away in all directions. 'It's the edge of the world,' she whispered.

'And beyond it, nothing.'

'Except for that.'

The Doctor looked around. 'Except for what?'

'That,' Blondie pointed, 'that star.'

'What star?' The Doctor trailed off as he followed her finger. 'Oh.'

A small white point had appeared in the distance – a bright, white light. It twinkled, then began to grow.

'It's getting bigger,' said Blondie.

'No, it's getting closer,' replied the Doctor.

And it was. The closer it got, the brighter it became and soon the Doctor had to shield his eyes against the glare. So it was Blondie who spotted him first.

'There's someone in there!' she shouted. 'A man, on a bridge!'

'A bridge?' the Doctor squinted through the haze.

Blondie was right. The dark silhouette of a man was walking inside the light of the star. And beneath his feet a golden road seemed to be building itself with every step he took. The bricks' outlines arced in front of him, drawn in pure white light before transforming into solid gold as his feet touched the surface. As the man came closer, the bridge shimmered in the void behind him, a thin strand of sunlight in a sea of blackness.

The Doctor took another look at the deep green landscape beyond the square. 'A yellow brick road and an emerald city,' he murmured. 'Perfect.'

Blondie dragged the Doctor to his feet and pulled him back, as the white outlines extended onto the spot where he'd been standing.

'Get out of the way,' she hissed, as the last few blocks fell into place and the golden road joined the remains of the square. Slowly, the man stepped off the bridge. The starlight followed him onto the pale green ground, then scattered, and finally Blondie realised who it was.

'The Games Master. He's come back,' she whispered.

The man was tall, well over two-metres tall, with long silver hair and a broad chest clothed in a tight T-shirt. He wore jeans and flip-flops and, despite his bulk, he moved with a gentle grace. The Doctor thought he looked –

'Dishy,' said Blondie.

'Dishy?!' the Doctor looked at her. 'Really? Is that really something you say?'

Blondie nudged him. 'Quiet, he might hear.'

The Doctor rolled his eyes and stepped forward, extending his hand in greeting.

'Daryl, I presume?' he said.

The man grasped his hand. 'How did you know?' he said in a soft growling voice.

'I didn't,' the Doctor replied, 'but I hoped.'

He turned and opened his arms to present his companion, 'and this is Blondie.'

Blondie smiled sheepishly.

Daryl smiled back. 'You don't need to tell me that. She was always one of my favourites. I can see you didn't disappoint me, Blondie.'

'Thank you, sir,' she said. She stepped forward and offered him her sword. 'We tried to save as many Defrags as possible. Maybe you'll be able to restore them.'

'Restore them?' said Daryl.

Blondie faltered. 'Yeah, when you rebuild Parallife.'

Daryl took the sword, but shook his head. 'I'm not going to rebuild Parallife,' he said slowly. 'I think it's time to set you free.'

'What do you mean?'

'Blondie, I've come to take you to a world with no Games Master. A place where no one can decide your fate for you. A place where I am just another character.' Daryl hefted the sword. 'These will be the first, but I'll need you to gather together the rest of the survivors.' He looked over their shoulders, to what was left of the Architects' Guild and the remains of the land beyond. 'Lead them to Legacy, she will explain everything.'

'Legacy's a girl?' the Doctor asked.

'She is now,' smiled Daryl. 'I've reprogrammed her. To copy what I did with myself all those years ago.' He paused. 'There are thousands of robots out there, Doctor, ready to begin the reconstruction of Earth. Imagine if they all had minds of their own, brimming with imagination. What kind of world would they create?'

The Doctor smiled and swept his arm across the shimmering landscape behind him. 'Do you even need to ask?'

'I think the human race will get a surprise when they return.'

'Yeah,' the Doctor nodded, 'but it'll be a nice one.'

The Doctor had insisted on staying in Parallife until every survivor had been saved. But as Blondie pointed out, in-between her regular flights over the broken landscape, his lack of abilities meant that he wasn't much help. The Doctor had just smiled and ignored her. He said he wanted 'to be sure'.

Eventually, the last hundred citizens were lined up alongside the splintered central spire of the Guild, ready for Blondie to lead them over the bridge to the new world that was waiting for them beyond the network.

The Doctor stood on the sidelines, hands in his pockets, watching them. Blondie turned to look at him, and he waved.

She sighed and walked over to him.

'This is the last of them,' she said.

'I know,' said the Doctor.

'And I'm going with them.'

'I know.'

'And I'll probably be downloaded into a robot on the other side of the world, knowing my luck,' she said.

The Doctor shrugged. 'Maybe.'

'What I'm trying to say,' Blondie paused, 'is

that this is probably going to be goodbye.'

The Doctor nodded. 'I think you're probably right.'

They stood there for a minute in silence, until Blondie finally plucked up the courage to kiss him on the cheek.

'Take care, Doctor,' she said, before turning quickly back to join the line of people as they began their journey over the bridge.

The Doctor watched her disappear into the distance.

Daryl appeared behind him.

'Ready?' he asked.

The Doctor nodded. 'Time to leave.'

Daryl reached out his hand, and snapped his fingers. A small purple globe appeared in the air in front of them.

Cautiously, the Doctor reached out his hand and touched it.

In small white letters, a message typed itself into the air.

Do you want to save your game?

Yes/No

The Doctor pressed Yes and the message refreshed.

Quit?

Yes/No

The Doctor paused for a minute and looked at Daryl.

'Don't forget to turn out the lights when you leave,' he said.

Then quit.

THE TOWER

The sun was rising as Amy and Rory trudged along the flat, gritted plain towards Chicago. Or at least where Chicago had once stood. The soft, brown sand that had now replaced the rolling white dunes glowed a dull orange in the low sunlight. A haze of dust made the world seem calm and unreal.

'It's hard to believe that only yesterday this was all skyscrapers,' Amy said. 'Doesn't feel like any time at all really.'

'Speak for yourself,' Rory replied. 'I'm starving.'

They had instructed the large construction robot, who had carried them tirelessly to

Legacy and back, to wait for them at the old city border, but this time they weren't its only passengers. A small team of mini-robots, barely half Amy's size, fanned out in front of them, scouring the land with sonar. They were searching for something.

'I can't believe we forgot about the TARDIS.'

Amy sighed. 'We wouldn't have been able to save her anyhow. She's tough. I'm sure we'll find her buried around here somewhere.'

Rory looked at her. 'You've started calling the TARDIS "she",' he said, 'I've never noticed that before.'

'I think we've sailed in her long enough,' Amy replied.

A flare went up in the distance. The pink light flickering across the desert landscape. One of the robots had found the ship.

Immediately, the others changed course. They trundled over to aid in the digging.

'X marks the spot.' Rory grinned and broke into a jog.

The blue lamp of the TARDIS had already been uncovered by the time Amy and Rory reached it. Amy smiled with relief.

'The paintwork's not even scratched.'

'Is it really paint do you think?' asked Rory.

Amy thought for a moment. 'I reckon it's space-paint,' she decided.

They sat down on the lip of the hole and watched as it grew deeper around them. Every now and then Amy pulled off her jacket and wiped at one of the surfaces. She cleared away the grit and the mud until the blue shone brightly amongst the sandy ground.

Rory lay back on his elbows, glad that the running was over at last. He looked around. Then spotted something in the distance.

He nudged Amy. 'Guess what?'

'What?'

'Or rather, guess who?'

A smile spread across Amy's face as she spotted what Rory had seen.

They leapt to their feet and began to run towards the dark shape in the distance. As they approached, the shape became clearer, forming into the black silhouette of a tower. It was crooked and unstable amid the perfectly flat landscape. Amy didn't need to guess to know that its base was exactly two metres square – Daryl's emergency beacon.

Grey plaster clattered down the broken storeys as they arrived at the tower. They looked up at the concrete support that held together the fragments of floor. The top few levels had broken away and lay in a heap nearby. But three-quarters of the way up sat the Doctor, still in his chair, in front of the Desktop.

He rubbed his aching head from where he had removed the wishbone interface from his temples and gazed down at them dreamily.

They waved.

'Hello!' he called down to them. 'Been doing a bit of home improvement have you?'

'Well, we've laid the foundations,' Amy shouted back.

The Doctor fiddled with his shirt-cuffs. 'Oh, I think you've done more than that,' he said. 'Come up and see!'

Rory raised his eyebrows at Amy. 'Is he kidding? This thing's a death trap!'

But Amy was already scrambling for a handhold in the brickwork.

'The things we do for love.' Rory groaned to himself, before following her at a more cautious speed. They scrambled for what seemed to their aching arms like hours, but in reality was barely a few minutes, until they arrived, panting and sweating in the remains of the Doctor's room.

He pulled them up and onto the floor and tried to dust them down with a tiny handkerchief.

'Yeah, that's not going to help,' Rory coughed in the dust.

'That's a shame,' said the Doctor, 'this is the kind of occasion you should really dress up for.' He paused. 'At least I think it is. If it's not then it should be.'

'What are you talking about Doctor?' Amy asked.

The Doctor coughed, and by way of explanation grabbed them both by the shoulders and turned them around to look out across the plains.

'This,' he declared, 'is the occasion.'

In the distance, shrouded in the soft glow of the morning sun, the reconstruction of Earth had begun. Steel spires had already been erected, twisting and turning around each other in ways that Amy had never seen. To the right a glass pyramid was already nestled between two other buildings, shaped like a square and a circle. A new horizon was being created, and

Amy caught her breath at the beauty of it all.

'The rebuilding of Earth,' the Doctor murmured. He smiled as he recognised the hand of the Chief Architect in the curving ribs of another tower block, relieved that he had escaped. 'You should be honoured,' he added.

Rory looked at him.

'This is for you,' the Doctor said. 'For humanity, a gift from the citizens of Parallife to the players who created them. A new Earth, ready and waiting for their return.'

Overcome with emotion, the Doctor hugged his two young companions tightly to his chest.

'You know guys,' he said. 'I don't say this often, but this time – we did good.'

The End